Sarah Mayberry

HOT ISLAND NIGHTS

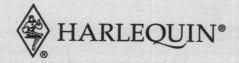

HARLEQUIN®

TORONTO • NEW YORK • LONDON
AMSTERDAM • PARIS • SYDNEY • HAMBURG
STOCKHOLM • ATHENS • TOKYO • MILAN • MADRID
PRAGUE • WARSAW • BUDAPEST • AUCKLAND

Recycling programs
for this product may
not exist in your area.

ISBN-13: 978-0-373-79570-3

HOT ISLAND NIGHTS

ABOUT THE AUTHOR

Sarah Mayberry lives in Melbourne, Australia—at the moment! With something like eight moves in the past ten years under her belt, she always keeps the cardboard boxes and packing tape within easy reach. When she's not moving or planning to move, she's writing, reading, cooking or trying to get motivated to do some exercise. Oh, and she loves a good movie night. By the time you read this, she also hopes that she will have become a dog owner.

Books by Sarah Mayberry

HARLEQUIN BLAZE
380—BURNING UP
404—BELOW THE BELT
425—AMOROUS LIAISONS
464—SHE'S GOT IT BAD
517—HER SECRET FLING

HARLEQUIN SUPERROMANCE
1551—A NATURAL FATHER
1599—HOME FOR
        THE HOLIDAYS
1626—HER BEST FRIEND

Huge thanks go to Pamela Torrance for giving up her time in the midst of her own upheaval to offer me pointers on what English people sound like. Thanks for the reality check, Pamela—consider the front end "your" part of the book!

As always, this book would not exist without the support of Chris, the heart, backbone and brain of my life. And, of course, Wanda, who never fails to knock me into shape and curb my excesses and cheer me toward the finishing line. Bless you!

1

ELIZABETH MASON STARED at the wedding registry in her hand. Printed on expensive linen paper beneath the green and gold Harrods logo, it was a roll call of prestigious brand names: Villeroy & Boch, Royal Doulton, Lalique, Noritake, Le Creuset. There were two dinner sets listed—one for everyday use, one for entertaining—cookware, stemware, cutlery, a champagne bucket, various pieces of barware, vases, platters, table linens...

If their wedding guests bought even half the items listed, she and Martin would have a house full of finely crafted, beautiful things with which to start their married life. Their home would be a showpiece, perfect in every detail.

Elizabeth pressed a hand to her chest. The tight feeling was back. As though she couldn't get enough air. She lowered her head and concentrated on regulating her breathing.

In, out. In, out.

A delicate piano sonata trickled over the sound system. A salesman brushed past, directing a customer to the Royal Worcester display. A bead of perspiration ran down Elizabeth's side.

She had to get a grip on these panic attacks. This was supposed to be a happy time. In eight weeks she would be marrying the man she'd been dating for the past six years and starting a new life with him. She shouldn't be feeling panicky or anxious.

"These are lovely, Elizabeth."

Elizabeth looked up to see her grandmother holding a glass from the Waterford Crystal collection. Light fractured off the highly polished surface of a champagne flute that appeared to be an exact replica of the set her grandparents had at home.

"They're beautiful," Elizabeth said. "But I think Martin prefers a more modern look. He's very keen on the Riedel flutes."

She could feel heat creeping into her face. She'd always been a terrible liar. *She* was the one who preferred the more modern design—Martin didn't give a fig about glassware. But she could hardly come right out and state her preference.

"Have a closer look, see how they feel in your hand," her grandmother said, gesturing for Elizabeth to join her.

Elizabeth opened her mouth to reiterate her objection—then closed it without saying a word. She knew what would happen once her grandmother realized Elizabeth didn't share her taste. Grandmama wouldn't say anything, of course, because it wasn't her way to express displeasure so directly, but her mouth would turn down at the corners and she'd be withdrawn for the rest of the day. She might not come to dinner, or perhaps there would be some mention of her heart medication.

It was emotional blackmail, of course, something Grandmama was a master at. Over the years she'd shaped Elizabeth's decisions and actions—major and minor—with the merest flutter of a hand or the mention of a headache or a doctor's visit. Even though Elizabeth understood the manipulation behind the behavior, she'd always given in. It was easier that way—and, really, at the end of the day, did it matter if she and Martin drank from the Waterford glasses instead of the Riedels if it made her grandmother happy?

So instead of standing her ground, she joined her grandmother and held the glass and agreed that it had a very pleasing weight in the hand, perfect for special occasions. Her grandmother collared a saleswoman and began asking questions about the manufacturing process and whether it would be possible to order replacement glasses in the future should any breakages occur.

Elizabeth stood to one side with a small, polite smile on her face. Around her, sales staff glided amongst the displays, talking in hushed, reverential tones. Everywhere she looked there were exquisite, fragile, priceless things, arranged to appeal to even the most fastidious eye.

Her gaze fell on a nearby table of cut-glass whiskey decanters. She had a vision of herself grabbing the table and upending the whole damn thing, sending the decanters smashing to the ground. It was so real her hands curled as though they were already gripping the table edge, and she could almost hear the crash of breaking glass and the shocked cries of the staff and customers.

She took a step backward and gripped her hands together.

Not because she thought there was any danger of her actually upending the display. There was no way she'd ever do such a thing.

She took another step away.

It's just prewedding jitters, she told herself. *Nothing to worry about. Every bride feels this way before her wedding.*

Except this wasn't the only reckless, anarchic impulse she'd had to quell recently. At last week's Friends of the Royal Academy luncheon she'd had to stifle the urge to throw back her head and scream at the top of her lungs when old Mr.

Lewisham had droned on about the quality of the napkins in the Academy's coffee shop and what it said about "society's declining standards." And yesterday she'd found her steps slowing outside a tattoo parlor near King's Cross station, admiring the tribal rose motif snaking up the arm of the girl behind the counter. She'd actually taken a step inside the store before common sense had reasserted itself and she'd remembered who she was.

"Elizabeth. Did you hear a word I just said?" her grandmother asked.

Elizabeth snapped into focus. Both the saleswoman and her grandmother were watching her, waiting for her response.

"Sorry, Grandmama, I was daydreaming," she said.

Her grandmother patted her arm fondly. "Come and have a look at the Wedgwood."

Smile fixed firmly in place, Elizabeth allowed herself to be led away.

It was late afternoon by the time she returned to her grandparents' Georgian town house in Mayfair. Her grandmother had come back after lunch for her afternoon rest, leaving Elizabeth to keep her appointment with the florist on her own. Elizabeth had dropped in to visit her friend Violet's boutique in Notting Hill on the way home and the hall clock was chiming six as she entered the house. She let her bag slide down her arm and started pulling off her scarf and gloves.

It was Tuesday, which meant Martin would be arriving any minute. He always ate here on Tuesday night. Just as he always played squash on Wednesdays and took her out for dinner on Fridays. If she hurried, she'd have time to freshen up before he arrived.

The housekeeper had stacked Elizabeth's mail neatly on the hall table and she flicked through it quickly as she turned toward the stairs. An official-looking envelope caught her eye and she paused. Martin had asked her to order a copy of her birth certificate so he could apply for their marriage license, since he was unable to request the certificate on her behalf. She tore the envelope open to confirm that it had finally arrived. One more thing to cross off her to-do list.

She unfolded the single sheet of paper, glancing over it quickly to check everything was in order. Elizabeth Jane Mason, born August 24, 1980, mother's name Eleanor Mary Whittaker, father's name—

Her scarf and gloves slipped from her fingers to the hall floor as she stared at the name beneath the box clearly marked Father's Given Name and Surname.

Sam Blackwell.

Who the hell is Sam Blackwell?

Her father was John Alexander Mason. Born January 16, 1942, killed in the same light-plane accident as her mother twenty-three years ago.

This had to be a mistake. It had to be.

Elizabeth focused on the closed door at the end of the long hallway. She started walking, certificate in hand, an uncomfortable tightness in her belly.

The sound of low, masculine laughter could be heard from behind the door of her grandfather's study as she drew closer, but for the first time in her life she didn't bother to knock.

"There's been some kind of mistake," she said as she barged into the room.

"Elizabeth. I was wondering when you'd get home," Martin said.

Her fiancé stood and approached to kiss her, his gray eyes crinkling at the corners as he smiled. As usual he was dressed immaculately in a tailored three-piece suit and conservatively striped silk tie, his dark hair parted neatly.

Instead of offering her mouth for his kiss, she thrust the certificate at him.

"Look. They've made a mistake. They've got my father's name wrong on my birth certificate."

For a split second Martin stilled. Then he shot her grandfather a quick, indecipherable look before turning his attention to the birth certificate.

"I thought you were going to have this delivered to the office so I could take care of the marriage license." Martin spoke mildly, but there was an undercurrent of tension in his voice.

Elizabeth looked at him, then at her grandfather's carefully blank face, and she knew.

It wasn't a mistake.

"What's going on?" Her voice sounded strange, wobbly and high.

"Why don't you have a seat, Elizabeth?" her grandfather suggested.

She allowed herself to be ushered into one of the button-back leather chairs facing the formidable mahogany desk. Her grandfather waited until Martin had taken the other seat before speaking.

"There is no mistake, I'm afraid. The man you know as your father, John Mason, was actually your stepfather. He married your mother when you were two years old."

For a moment there was nothing but the sound of the clock ticking. Elizabeth started to speak, then stopped because she had no idea what to say.

She'd been devastated by her parents' deaths when she was seven years old. For the first few months she'd lived with her grandparents she'd cried herself to sleep every night. She treasured the small mementos she had of her childhood—the vintage Steiff teddy bear her parents had given her when she was four, the rock fossils they'd found together on a family holiday, the empty perfume bottle that had once held her mother's favorite scent.

But now her grandfather was telling her that her parents weren't both dead, that it was her stepfather who'd died. That her real father—the stranger whose name was listed on her birth certificate—might still be alive and well somewhere in the world.

"Why has no one ever told me this before?"

"Because it wasn't necessary. I won't go into details, but Sam Blackwell is not someone we want involved in your life. John Mason was your father in every other way, so we didn't see the point in bringing up something that was best forgotten," her grandfather said.

There were so many assumptions in his speech, so many judgments. And all of them made on her behalf, with no consultation with her whatsoever.

Elizabeth's hands curled into fists. "Is he alive? My real father?"

"I believe so, yes."

She leaned forward. "Where does he live? What does he do? Is he in London? How can I contact him?"

"Elizabeth, I know this is a shock for you, but when you've had a chance to process I'm sure you'll agree that it really doesn't change your life in any substantial way," Martin said.

Elizabeth focussed on Martin for the first time. "You knew."

"Your grandfather told me after I proposed."

"You've known for *six months* and you didn't tell me?"

"Don't be angry with Martin. I requested that he respect my confidence. I didn't see the point in getting you upset over nothing," her grandfather said.

Nothing? *Nothing?*

"I'm thirty years old. I don't need to be protected. I deserve the truth. And my father being alive is not *nothing*. It is very decidedly *something*."

Martin shifted uncomfortably. Her grandfather placed his hands flat on the leather blotter on his desk and eyed her steadily.

"We did what we thought was best for you."

This was usually the point in any argument with her grandparents when she retreated. They'd taken her in when her parents died and bent over backward to ensure she had a happy childhood. They'd sent her to the best schools, attended every school play and recital and parent-teacher night, taken her on holidays to France and Italy—all despite her grandmother's heart condition and frail health. Elizabeth had grown up with a strong sense of obligation toward them and a determination that she would never be more of a burden than she had to be.

She'd excelled at school, then at university. She'd never stayed out late or come home drunk. She'd never had a one-night stand. Even her husband-to-be had come with their seal of approval, since he worked at her grandfather's law firm.

She owed them so much—everything, really. But she also owed herself. And what they'd done was wrong.

"This was my decision to make. You had no right to keep this from me."

Because she didn't trust herself to say more, because rage and a bunch of unwise, unruly words were pressing at the back of her throat, she stood and left the room. She'd barely made it halfway up the hall when she heard Martin coming after her.

"Elizabeth. Slow down."

He caught her elbow. She spun on him, pulling her arm free.

"Don't you dare tell me to calm down or that this doesn't matter, Martin. Don't you dare."

Her chest was heaving with the intensity of her emotions and he took a step away, clearly taken aback by her ferocity.

"If I could have told you without breaking your grandfather's confidence, I would have. Believe me." He was deeply sincere, his eyes worried.

"You're my fiancé, Martin. Don't you think you owe your loyalty to me before my grandfather?"

He ran a hand through his hair. "Under ordinary circumstances, yes, but your grandfather and I have a professional relationship as well as a personal one."

"I see." And she did. Martin was hoping to be made partner at the firm this year. The last thing he wanted was to rock the boat.

He reached out and took her hand, his thumb brushing reassuringly across her knuckles. "Elizabeth, if we could go somewhere private and talk this through, I'm sure you'll understand that everything was done with your best interests at heart."

Her incredulous laughter sounded loud in the hall.

"My best interests? How on earth would you know what my best interests are, Martin? You're so busy telling me what's good for me, you have no idea who I am or what I really want. It's like those bloody awful Waterford champagne flutes. No one cares what I think, and I'm such a pathetic coward I swallow it and swallow it and swallow it, even while I tell myself it's because I want to do the right thing and not upset the applecart."

Martin frowned. "Champagne flutes? I have no idea what you're talking about."

She knew he didn't, but it was all inextricably entwined in her head: her anger at her grandparents and Martin for this huge betrayal of her trust, her feelings of frustration and panic over the wedding, the suffocated feeling she got every time her grandparents made a decision for her or Martin spoke to her in that soothing tone and treated her as though she were made of fine porcelain.

"I can't do this," she said, more to herself than him. "This is a mistake."

It was suddenly very clear to her.

Martin slid his arm around her shoulders, trying to draw her into a hug. "Elizabeth, you're getting yourself upset."

The feeling of his arms closing so carefully around her was the last straw. She braced her hands against his chest and pushed free from his embrace.

"I want to call off the wedding."

Martin blinked, then reached for her again. "You don't mean that. You're upset."

She held him off. "Violet has been saying for months that I should stop and think about what I'm doing, and she's right. I don't want this, Martin. I feel like I'm suffocating."

"Violet. I might have known she'd have something to do with this. What rubbish has she been filling your head with now? The joys of being a free and easy slapper in West London? Or maybe how to get a head start on cirrhosis?"

He'd never liked Violet, which was only fair, since her best friend had taken a violent aversion to him from the moment they'd first met.

"No, actually. She pointed out that I was going to be thirty this year and that if I didn't wake up and smell the coffee I'd be fifty and still living the life my grandparents chose for me."

"What a load of rubbish."

She looked at him, standing there in his Savile Row suit, his bespoke shirt pristine-white. He didn't understand. Maybe he couldn't.

She knew about his childhood, about the poverty and the sacrifices his working-class single mom had made to send him to university. Elizabeth's life—the life they were supposed to have together once they were married—was the fulfillment of all his aspirations. The high-paying partnership with the long-established law firm, the well-bred wife to come home to, the holidays on the French or Italian Riviera, membership at all the right men's clubs.

"We can't get married, Martin. You don't know who I am," she said quietly. "How could you? *I* don't even know who I am."

She turned and walked up the hallway.

"Elizabeth. Can we at least talk about this?"

She kept walking. Her grandparents were going to be upset when they heard she'd called off the wedding. It wouldn't simply be a case of her grandmother having a headache—this would instigate full-scale damage control. They'd use every trick in the book to try to make her see sense. They'd make her feel guilty and stupid and wrong without actually accusing her of being any of those things. And she was so used to not rocking the boat, to toeing the line and doing the right thing that she was terribly afraid that she might listen to them and wind up married to Martin and unpacking all those expensive Harrods housewares in her marital home.

She needed some time to herself. To think. To work things out. Somewhere private and quiet. She thought of Violet's apartment above her shop and quickly discarded it. Even if it wasn't only a one bedroom, she wouldn't find much peace and quiet in Violet's hectic world. Plus it would be the first place her grandparents would look for her. Then she remembered what she'd said to Martin—*I don't even know who I am*—and the answer came to her.

She would go to her father. Wherever he might be. She would find him, and she would go to him, and she would start working out who Elizabeth Jane Mason really was, and what she really wanted.

FOUR DAYS LATER, ELIZABETH OPENED her rental car window and sucked in big lungfuls of fresh air. Her eyes were gritty with fatigue and she opened them wide, willing herself to wakefulness. She'd been traveling for nearly thirty hours to reach the other side of the world and now the foreign, somber-hued scrub of rural Australia was rushing past as she drove southwest from Melbourne toward Phillip Island, a small dot on the map nestled in the mouth of Westernport Bay.

She'd spent the past few days holed up in a hotel room in Soho while Violet leaned on her police-officer cousin to use his contacts to locate Elizabeth's father. The moment she'd learned that Sam Blackwell's last known place of residence was Phillip Island in Victoria, Australia, Elizabeth had booked a room at a local hotel and jumped on a plane.

She hadn't spoken to her grandparents beyond assuring them she was fine and perfectly sane and determined to stand by her decision to cancel the wedding. Her grandfather had tried to talk her out of it over the phone, of course, but she'd cut the conversation short.

Whatever happened next in her life was going to be her decision and no one else's.

The San Remo bridge appeared in front of her and she drove over a long stretch of water. Then she was on the island and the thought of meeting her father, actually looking into his face and perhaps seeing an echo of her own nose or eyes or cheekbones, chased the weariness away.

She had no idea what to expect from this meeting. She wasn't even sure what she wanted from it. A sense of connection? Information about where she came from? A replacement for the parents she'd lost when she was only seven years old?

The truth was, she could hardly remember her mother and father—or the man she knew as her father. There were snatches of memory—her mother laughing, the smell of her stepfather's pipe tobacco, moments from a family holiday—but precious little else. Her mother was always slightly sad in her few clear memories, her stepfather distant. Despite her lack of recall—or, perhaps, because of it—she'd always felt as though something profound was missing in her life. Her grandparents had been kind and loving in their own way, but their careful guardianship had not filled the gap the loss of her parents had left in her heart.

A gap she'd never fully acknowledged until right this minute. It was only now that she was on the verge of meeting her biological father for the first time that she understood how much she'd always craved the wordless, instinctive connection between parent and child, how she'd envied her friends their relationships with their parents.

Her hands tightened on the steering wheel and she gave herself a mental pep talk as she drove into the tree-lined main street of the township of Cowes, the most densely populated township on the island. It was highly likely that her father didn't even know she existed. Arriving on his doorstep full of expectations was the best way to start off on the wrong foot. She needed to be realistic and patient. They were strangers. There was no reason to think that they would feel any special connection with each other, despite the fact that they shared DNA.

And yet her stomach still lurched with nervousness as she turned the corner onto her father's street and stopped out the front of a cream and Brunswick-green house that had all the architectural appeal of a shoe box. Clad in vertical aluminum siding, it featured a flat roof, a deep overhang over a concrete porch, sliding metal windows and a patchy, brown front lawn.

A far cry from the elegant, historically listed homes of Mayfair. She wiped her suddenly sweaty hands on the thighs of her trousers.

She had no idea what kind of man her father was. What sort

of life he'd led. How he might react to his long-lost daughter appearing on his doorstep.

She'd had a lot of time to think about what might have happened between her mother and father all those years ago. In between dodging phone calls from Martin and reassuring her grandparents, she'd made some inquiries. She'd discovered that John Mason and her mother had married in January 1982 when Elizabeth was seventeen months old—further proof, if she'd been looking for it, that the birth certificate was accurate and John was not her father.

What the marriage record couldn't tell her was when her stepfather and mother had met or how long they'd dated before they got married or if there had been another man on the scene at the time. Her father, for example.

Her grandfather clearly didn't have a great opinion of Sam Blackwell. She wondered what her father had done to earn his condemnation. She'd been tempted to confront her grandfather again before she departed and insist he tell her everything he knew, but after a great deal of debating she'd decided not to. She was going to meet her father and talk to him and hear his story and form her own opinion about him.

But before she did any of that, she needed to get her backside out of the car and across the lawn to her father's front door.

She didn't move.

Come on, Elizabeth. You didn't fly all this way to sit in a hire car out the front of your father's house like some sort of deranged stalker.

And yet she still didn't reach for the door handle.

This meant so much to her. A chance to feel connected to someone. A chance to have a father.

Just do it, Elizabeth.

She curled her fingers around the cool metal of the door

handle just as her phone rang, the sound shrill in the confines of the car. She checked caller ID.

"Violet," she said as she took the call.

"E. How was your flight? What's happening? Have you spoken to him yet?"

"Long. Not much. And no," Elizabeth said, answering her friend's questions in order. "I'm sitting in front of his house right now, trying to get up the courage to knock on the door."

"You're nervous."

"Just a little."

"Don't be. Once he gets to know you, he'll be over the moon you've tracked him down."

Elizabeth pulled a face. Violet's vote of confidence was lovely, but if her father knew she existed—a big *if*—he'd clearly had his reasons for keeping his distance for the past thirty-odd years.

"I don't know. Maybe I'm doing this all wrong." Elizabeth studied the slightly shabby house doubtfully. "Maybe I should have made contact with a letter or e-mail first. Used a lawyer to break the ice…"

"No. You've done the right thing. And even if you haven't, you're there now. All you have to do is knock on his door."

"You make it sound so easy," Elizabeth joked.

"Come on, E. You're a woman on a mission, remember? You're reclaiming your life, striking out on your own. Shaking off old Droopy Drawers was just the first step."

Elizabeth frowned at her friend's less-than-flattering description of Martin. "I wish you wouldn't call him that. Just because I've decided not to marry him doesn't mean he's a bad person."

"True. It's not as though he's going around *literally* boring people to death. Although he took a fairly good stab at stifling the life out of you."

"Vi…"

"Sorry. I just think it should be a punishable offense for someone as young as he is to carry on like a crusty old bugger. How many thirty-two-year-olds do you know wear cardigans with leather elbow patches?"

"Just because he dresses conservatively doesn't mean he's crusty, Vi. He's just…conservative," Elizabeth finished lamely.

"*Conservative?* I'm sorry, E, but conservative is not the word for a man who refuses to have sex in anything other than the missionary position. The word you're looking for is *repressed.*"

Elizabeth kneaded her forehead with the tips of her fingers. "You have no idea how much I regret ever saying anything to you about that, Vi."

Martin would be mortified if he knew that she'd discussed their sex life with anyone. Especially Violet.

Elizabeth blamed her dentist. If it hadn't been for the stupid article in the stupid women's magazine in his waiting room, there was no way she would have tried to talk to Martin about her "sexual needs and desires" instead of "vainly waiting for him to intuit" them, and there was no way she would have felt the need to seek counsel from her best friend in the embarrassing aftermath.

"I'm not going to apologize for refusing to let you sweep that sterling little moment under the rug," Violet said. "*Normal* people—note I'm stressing the word *normal,* as opposed to *uptight repressives*—talk to each other about sex and explore their sexuality and have fun in bed. They don't pat you on the head and tell you they respect you too much to objectify you, or whatever rubbish excuse he came out with after you'd finally got up the gumption to talk to him. And I love that he tried to make it all about you, by the way, and not about his hang-ups."

"I really don't want to talk about this again."

But Violet was off and running on one of her favorite rants. "For God's sake, it wasn't as though you asked him to tie you up and go at you with a cheese grater or something. You wanted to do it doggy style, big bloody deal. There were no small animals involved, no leather or hot wax."

"I've called off the wedding, Vi. This is definitely filed under The Past. You need to let it go."

There was a small silence on the other end of the phone.

"You're right. Sorry. He just really gets on my wick."

"Well, you'll probably never have to see him again, since he's hardly going to want to know me once he's gotten over the fact that I've dumped him. That should make you feel better."

A dart of fear raced down Elizabeth's spine as she registered her own words. She'd changed the course of her life by walking away from the wedding and she had no idea what might happen next. A terrifying, knee-weakening thought. But she refused to regret her decision. The truth was she'd never really loved Martin the way a woman should love the man with whom she planned to spend the rest of her life. She was fond of him. She admired his many good qualities. He made her feel safe. But he also exasperated her and made her yearn for...*something* she didn't even have a name for.

"E. Someone's just come into the shop and I have to go. But you can do this, okay? Just get out of the car and go introduce yourself. Whatever comes after that, you'll handle it."

"Thanks, coach. And thanks for all the hand-holding and tissue-passing and intel-gathering over the past few days," Elizabeth said.

"Pshaw," her friend said before ending the call.

Elizabeth put her phone in her handbag and took a deep

breath. It was time to stop fannying about and get this over and done with.

Her heart in her mouth, she opened the car door and stepped into the hot Australian sun.

2

NATHAN JONES WOKE TO a single moment of pure nothingness. For a split second before the forgetfulness of sleep fell away, he felt nothing, knew nothing, remembered nothing.

It was the best part of his day, hands down.

And then he woke fully and it was all there: the memories, the anxiety, the guilt and shame and fear. Heavy and relentless and undeniable.

He stared at the ceiling for a long beat, wondering at the fact that he kept forcing himself to jump through the flaming hoop of this shit, day in, day out. There was precious little joy in it and plenty of pain.

Then he forced himself to sit up and swing his legs over the side of the bed. It wasn't like he had a choice, after all. He wasn't a quitter. Even though there were times when it seemed damned appealing.

His head started throbbing the moment he was upright. He breathed deeply. It would pass soon enough. God knew he'd chalked up enough experience dealing with hangovers over the past four months to know.

The important thing was that he hadn't woken once that he could remember. If the price he had to pay this morning for oblivion last night was a hangover, then so be it.

He stood and ran a hand over his hair, then grabbed the towel flung over the end of the bed and wrapped it around his waist. He worked his tongue around his mouth as he headed for the door. Water was called for. And maybe some food. Although he wasn't certain about the food part just yet.

The full glare of the midmorning sun hit him the moment he stepped out of the studio into the yard. He grunted and shielded his eyes with his forearm. Looked like it was going to be another stinker.

He crossed to the main house and entered the kitchen. The kitchen floor was gritty with sand beneath his feet and he smiled to himself. Sam would have a cow when he came home, no doubt. Nate had never met a guy more anal about keeping things shipshape and perfect. A regular Mr. Clean, was Sammy.

The fridge yielded a bottle of water and he closed his eyes, dropped his head back and tipped it down his throat. He swallowed and swallowed until his teeth ached from the cold, then put the nearly empty bottle onto the kitchen counter. He was about to head to the shower when a knock sounded at the front door.

Nate frowned. He wasn't expecting anyone. Didn't particularly want to see anyone, either. That was the whole point of being on the island—privacy. Peace and quiet. Space.

He walked through the living room to the front hallway. He could see a silhouette through the glass panel in the door. As he hovered, debating whether or not to answer, the silhouette lifted its hand and knocked again.

"Coming," he said, aware he sounded more than a little like a grumpy old man.

The door swung open and he found himself facing a tall, slim woman with delicately sculpted features and deep blue eyes, her pale blond hair swept up into the kind of hairstyle that made him think of Grace Kelly and other old-school movie stars.

"Yes?" he said, his tone even more brusque. Probably because he hadn't expected to find someone so beautiful on his front step.

She opened her mouth then closed it without saying anything as her startled gaze swept from his face to his chest, belly and south, then up to his bare chest again. There was a long, pregnant silence as she stared at his sternum. Then she pinned her gaze on a point just beyond his right shoulder and cleared her throat.

"I'm terribly sorry. I'm looking for Sam Blackwell. I was told this is his place of residence."

Her voice was clipped and cultured, the kind of cut-glass accent he associated with the royal family and people who maintained a string of polo ponies.

"You've got the right place, but Sam's not around right now," he said.

"I see. Could you tell me when he'll be back?" She darted a quick, nervous glance toward his chest before fixing her gaze over his shoulder again. If he didn't know better, he'd think she'd never seen a bare chest before, the way she couldn't bring herself to look him in the eye. Six months ago he would have been amused and intrigued by her flustered reaction—she was a beautiful woman, after all.

But that was six months ago.

"Sam won't be back until the new year," he said. "Try him again after the fifth or sixth."

He started to swing the door closed between them.

"The new year? But that's nearly a month away." Her eyes met his properly for the first time, wide with disbelief and maybe a little bit of dismay.

His gut told him to close the door, send her on her way.

He had enough on his plate without taking on someone else's worries.

"Not much I can do about that, sorry," he said instead.

She pushed a strand of hair off her forehead. The movement made her white linen shirt gape and he caught a glimpse of coffee-colored lace and silk.

"Do you have a number I can contact him at?"

"No offense, but I'm not about to hand Sam's number out to just anybody."

She blinked. "But I'm not just anybody, I assure you."

"If you want to leave your number and a message with me, I'll make sure he gets it."

She frowned. "This isn't the kind of thing you handle with a message."

Nate shrugged. He'd offered her a solution, but if she wasn't interested...

"Then maybe you need to wait till Sam's back in town."

"I've travelled thousands of miles to see him, Mr....?" She paused, waiting for him to supply his name.

"Nate. Nathan Jones."

"My name's Elizabeth Mason."

She held out her hand. After a second's hesitation he shook it. Her fingers were cool and slender, her skin very soft.

"I really need to make contact with Sam Rockwell," she said, offering what he guessed was her best social smile.

"Like I said, leave your number with me, and I'll make sure he gets it."

Her finely arched eyebrows came together in a frown. "Perhaps you could tell me where he is, then, if you won't give me his number?"

"Look, Ms. Mason, whatever this is about, if Sam owes you money or something else, the best I can do for you is to pass your number on. That's it, end of story."

"I'm not a debt collector." She appeared shocked at the idea.

"Whatever. That's my best offer, take it or leave it."

When she simply stared at him, he shrugged. "Fine," he said, and he started closing the door again.

"He's my father. Sam Blackwell is my father," she blurted.

That got his attention.

Sam had never mentioned a daughter, or any other family for that matter. Not that the omission necessarily meant anything, given that Sam wasn't exactly the talkative type.

Nate frowned. Why would Sam invite his daughter to visit when he knew he was going to be interstate?

"Sam didn't know you were coming, did he?"

"No, he didn't." She gave a nervous little laugh. "In fact, I suspect he doesn't even know I exist. Which makes me incredibly stupid to have jumped on a plane to come find him like this, but I didn't even think about the fact that he might not even be here—"

Nate took an instinctive step backward as her voice broke and tears filled her eyes.

Should have shut the door when you had the chance, buddy.

She tilted her head back and blinked rapidly. Nate considered and discarded a number of responses before reluctantly pushing the door wide.

"You'd better come in," he said.

She gave him a grateful look as she walked past him and into the house. He led her to the kitchen.

"You want some water?"

"Yes, thank you."

He waved her toward one of the beat-up vinyl upholstered chairs around the kitchen table, then grabbed a glass from the cupboard and filled it at the tap.

"Thank you," she said as he handed her the glass. "I promise I'm not normally like this. It's just that it's been a long flight and things have been a little crazy lately. And I really should have thought this through some more—" She shook her head. The hand holding the glass was trembling with emotion. "Sorry. I'm babbling again. I'm not normally a babbler, either."

She offered him a tremulous smile. She looked so vulnerable sitting there, so lost and confused.

Everything in Nate screamed retreat. He didn't need this.

"Look, I don't want to get involved in some kind of family dispute or *This Is Your Life* situation," he said.

Her smile disappeared as a deep flush rose up her neck and into her cheeks.

"I don't believe I asked you to get involved, Mr. Jones. I was simply conveying the facts of my situation to you."

"Well, if it's all the same to you, I'd rather not know even that."

"By all means." Chair legs scraped across the linoleum floor as she stood abruptly. "If you'd simply give me my father's number, I won't bother you a moment longer."

Nate reached for the pad and pen beside the phone and pushed them across the counter toward her.

"Give me your number, I'll make sure Sam gets it," he repeated.

She might be beautiful, she might even have what he suspected was a great ass under the expensive tailoring of her crumpled linen trousers, but he wasn't about to sic her on his old friend without some kind of warning.

She stared at him incredulously. "You're still not going to give me his contact details? Even after everything I've just told you?"

"Sam's my friend."

Her chest rose and fell as though she was fighting to restrain herself from saying something. Then her mouth firmed and her chin came up.

"Fine. Thank you for the water."

She turned toward the door.

"Aren't you forgetting something?" he said. He tapped the pen against the pad.

Her nostrils flared. Then, holding herself very upright, she strode to the kitchen counter and snatched the pen from his hand, writing her phone number in the elegant, curling strokes of a bygone era. When she was finished she dropped the pen onto the counter and lifted her chin even higher.

"I can see myself out, thank you," she said with enormous dignity.

"Where are you staying in town?"

"I fail to see how that's any of your business."

"In case your phone doesn't work for some reason, so I can leave a message for you," he explained patiently. Although he was fast running out of that particular commodity. He hadn't asked for Ms. Mason and her troubles to walk in the door.

"I'm sure it will be fine."

The look she gave him was so snooty, the tilt of her head so imperious he decided he'd done his good deed for the day.

"Fair enough. Don't blame me if I can't contact you for some reason."

A small muscle worked in her jaw. He had the distinct impression she was grinding her teeth.

"I'm staying at the Isle of Wight," she finally said.

"Duly noted."

She hovered for a second as though she didn't quite know what to do next, then she strode to the front door. She paused on the verge of exiting, looking back at him across the width of the living room.

"And by the way, Mr. Jones, where I come from it's good manners to put clothes on before receiving visitors," she said.

She was so hoity-toity, so on her dignity that Nate couldn't help himself—he laughed, the sound bursting out of him and echoing loudly off the walls. By the time he'd pulled himself together enough to notice, she was gone.

The smile slowly faded from his lips. It had been a long time since he'd laughed like that. A long time.

For no reason that he was prepared to acknowledge, he walked into the living room and pushed the curtain to one side. Despite her touch-me-not, refined air she had a sexy sway to her walk and he watched her ass the whole way to her car.

She opened the car and slid into the driver's seat, but didn't take off immediately. Instead, she simply sat there, her head lowered, her expression unreadable from this distance.

Trying to work out what to do next, he figured.

He told himself that she was none of his business, that he had more than enough shit to shovel in his own life, but he couldn't take his eyes off her. And he couldn't stop thinking about the way her hand had trembled when she held the glass of water. And how lost and scared she'd sounded under all that well-educated, well-enunciated hauteur.

"Bloody hell."

He grabbed a pair of board shorts from the laundry, tugged them on, then exited the house and walked down the hot concrete path toward her car. She didn't notice him approaching and she started when he rapped on the passenger window. She hesitated a second, then pressed the button to lower the glass.

"Look, Sam's in Sydney until the start of the race and won't get into Hobart until New Year's Eve at the soonest," he said. "But once he knows you're here, I'm sure he'll come straight back."

"Race? What race?"

"The Sydney to Hobart yacht race."

She bit her lip. "I've heard of that. Isn't it very dangerous?"

"Sam's an experienced sailor. One of the best."

"Is that what he does? Sail, I mean?"

"He hires out as crew mostly, and sometimes he delivers yachts for owners."

He took a step backward to signal the question-and-answer session was over. It wasn't his place to fill in the blanks for her. That was between father and daughter. Nothing to do with him.

"I'll let you know as soon as I've spoken to Sam," he said.

She hesitated, then nodded. The glass slid up between them and she started the car then pulled away from the curb.

Nate watched until she'd turned the corner. Guilt ate at him. He should have helped her more. Reassured her. She'd come a long way looking for a man she knew nothing about. He could have called Sam on the spot, told him—

Nate caught himself before he let the thought go any further. Since when had he made himself Elizabeth Mason's knight in shining armor?

He smiled grimly, the action more a show of teeth than anything else. Rescuing damsels in distress was hardly his forte, after all. Look what had happened to the last damsel who'd put her faith in him.

Tension banded his shoulders and chest. Pressure pushed at the back of his eyes and nose. His heart started to race as sweat prickled beneath his arms.

Olivia. Bloody, bloody hell.

He stared at the dry lawn beneath his feet, battling with himself. Then he strode toward the house and took the steps to the porch in one long-legged leap. Usually he tried not to drink before four o'clock, but trial and error had taught him that there was only one way to hold the anxiety at bay. He went straight to the kitchen and grabbed a can of beer from the fridge. He downed it quickly, closing his eyes and waiting for the alcohol to warm his belly. Vodka would be faster, of course, as would any other hard spirit. He wasn't sure why he clung to beer as his therapy of choice. The illusion that it still meant he had some self-control, perhaps?

Whatever. The tight feeling banding his chest eased and he reached for his second beer with less urgency.

After this, maybe he'd phone around, see who was heading out to Summerlands or one of the other surf beaches so he could catch a few waves. Kill a few hours before he could hit the pub at a more socially acceptable time and start drinking himself toward oblivion again.

And then another day would be over. One less trial to be faced. Hip, hip, hooray.

ELIZABETH STARED AT THE peeling paint on her hotel room ceiling. The sound of laughter and the hum of conversation drifted in the open window. She'd been trying to sleep for the past three hours, but the room she'd been assigned at the Isle of Wight Hotel boasted only an old oscillating fan to combat the heat. Even though she was lying in her underwear on top of the sheets it was like being in a sauna. A really noisy, loud sauna, thanks to the fact that her window looked out over the hotel's beer garden.

She was so tired she should have been able to sleep through a hurricane, but her mind was racing, going over and over the same ground. She didn't know what to do. Stay and wait for her father to come home? Go to Sydney and try to track him down somehow? Or—God forbid—return to England with her tail between her legs.

She hated the idea of having come all this way for nothing, but the idea of waiting and putting her trust in Nathan Jones was enough to fill her with despair.

She made an impatient sound and flopped onto her back. Every time she thought about Nathan Jones she got annoyed all over again. The way he'd told her straight up that he didn't trust her and that he didn't want to get involved in whatever was going on between her and her father. The way he'd shrugged so negligently when she'd been practically throwing herself on his mercy.

"Stupid beach-bum git," she muttered.

Because that was exactly what he was—a beach bum. He'd very obviously just rolled out of bed when he opened the door, even though it was nearly midday. His short, dark hair had been rumpled, his pale blue eyes bloodshot, and she'd caught a whiff of stale beer when she passed him on the way to the kitchen. It wasn't hard to guess what he'd been up to last night.

As for the way he'd stood around with nothing but a frayed towel hanging low on his hips and his ridiculously overdeveloped body on display…

She stirred, uneasy about the way images of his big, hard body kept sliding into her mind. The deeply tanned firmness of his shoulders. The trail of gold-tinted hair that bisected his hard belly and disappeared beneath the towel. The way his biceps had bulged when he crossed his arms over his chest.

The way he'd laughed at her when she'd reminded him that anyone with half-decent manners would have thrown some clothes on before inviting someone into his home.

She sat up and swung her legs to the floor.

Clearly, she wasn't going to get any sleep.

She crossed the threadbare carpet to where she'd left the shopping bags from her brief foray along Main Street earlier in the day. By the time she'd checked into her room her linen shirt had been damp beneath her armpits and perspiration had been running down the backs of her knees. She'd packed for an English summer, not an Australian one, and she'd quickly realized she would need to get a few items of lighter clothing if she was going to survive the next few days with her sanity intact. She'd bought herself a yellow-and-red sundress and a couple of pastel-colored tank tops. None of it was in her usual style—tailored, elegant—but it was light and breezy and much more suitable for the weather.

Now she pulled on the sundress and checked herself in the tarnished mirror on the back of the bathroom door. The skirt was a little shorter than she'd like—just above her knee—and the halter neck meant she couldn't wear a bra, but there was no doubting that the cotton fabric was blessedly cool compared to her own clothes.

She spent a few minutes coiling her hair into a neat chignon, then she checked her watch. Six o'clock. The whole evening stretched ahead of her, long and empty.

Maybe she should explore Main Street more thoroughly while the light lasted. Or perhaps she could walk along the jetty, maybe even along the beach…?

She crossed to the window to close it before she left the room and her gaze fell on the life and color and movement in the beer garden downstairs. There were dozens of holidaymakers clustered around tables, dressed in shorts and swimsuits and bright summer clothes, downing beer and wine and laughing with each other.

Every time she'd ever holidayed someplace warm she'd always been traveling with her grandparents or Martin. The sort of restaurants and hotels they favored were discreet and refined—a far cry from the raucous chaos on display down below.

A peal of laughter floated up through the window and Elizabeth found herself smiling instinctively in response.

If Violet was here, she'd go down and join in the fun, a little voice whispered in her ear.

Elizabeth frowned and pulled the window closed, flicking the lock into place.

She wasn't Violet. She couldn't just go downstairs and buy herself a drink and become part of the noise and the laughter. That simply wasn't the kind of person she was.

Who says? I thought this was about finding out who you really are, what you really want? Wouldn't going downstairs be part of that? the voice piped up again. Perhaps not very surprisingly, it sounded exactly like her best friend.

"You're a damned interfering nag, you know that?" she told her empty room.

But she knew the voice was right. She'd run away from her old life because she was afraid of the person she'd nearly become. If she was going to find herself, she needed to go looking. She needed to push against her old notions of who she was.

She grabbed her purse and her room key and made herself walk out the door before she could think herself out of it. Nerves fluttered in her belly as she descended the stairs and walked into the din of the crowded main bar. She paused for a moment to get her bearings, a little overwhelmed by the noise and the press of people and all the bare flesh on display. The smell of beer and fried food and suntan lotion hung heavily in the air, and the carpet underfoot was both sticky from years' worth of spilled drinks and gritty with sand that had been tracked in from the beach.

It's just a pub, Elizabeth, she told herself, *and they're just people. Nothing to be afraid of.*

She took a deep breath and threw herself into the melee, slowly weaving her way toward the bar.

"What can I get you, love?" the barmaid asked.

"I'll have a Pimm's and lemonade, thank you."

The barmaid frowned. "Pimm's. God, I haven't served that

for years." She turned toward the man working the other end of the scarred wooden bar. "Trev, we got any Pimm's, do you reckon?"

"Pimm's? I don't know. Let me check out the back." The barman glanced at Elizabeth curiously.

"It's okay, don't bother," Elizabeth said, feeling foolish. Of course they didn't have Pimm's. She was a long way from home, after all. About as far away as she could get.

She gestured toward the frosted glass the barmaid had just handed over to the previous customer. "I'll just have one of those."

"A VB? Not a problem," the barmaid said.

A minute later, Elizabeth was handed a tall, frosted glass full of beer. She took her first sip and gasped, surprised by how icy cold it was. After the heat of the day, however, it was hugely welcome and she took another big gulp as she spotted an empty table in the corner. Good. A table would give her a refuge to hide behind and make her feel less conspicuously alone.

She dodged a couple of well-muscled backs as she made her way across the bar. She was just about to put her drink down when a dark-haired woman slid her glass onto the table at the same time. They stared at each other, startled, then the other woman laughed.

"I'd call that a draw, what do you think? Should we toss for it?" the other woman said good-naturedly and Elizabeth recognized the familiar vowels of an East London accent.

"It's fine. You got here first," Elizabeth said politely.

It had been a mistake coming downstairs on her own, she could see that now. It was too loud, too hectic and she was jet-lagged and very uncertain about what move to make next. The sooner she drank her beer and returned to her room, the better.

"Hey! English! Cheers!" the other woman said, her face

splitting into a welcoming smile. She lifted her glass to clink it against Elizabeth's. "How long have you been in Oz for, then? Me and my bloke have been here nearly six months, in case you couldn't tell by the tan." The other woman proudly showed off her nut-brown arms. "Bugger skin cancer, I say." She gave another laugh.

Her name, Elizabeth soon learned, was Lexie and she insisted that she and Elizabeth share the table since Lexie was waiting for her boyfriend to join her and had no idea when he was going to show up.

"You can help me fight off these randy Aussie blokes until he gets here," she said with another of her loud, unselfconscious laughs. "Horny bastards, and they don't mind having a go, let me tell you, even when you let them know you're taken."

Somehow Elizabeth's one beer turned into two when Lexie insisted on treating her, then three because Elizabeth had to return the favor. By the time it was full dark outside she was feeling more than a little squiffy. By that time Lexie's boyfriend, Ross, had arrived with the rest of their friends and Elizabeth was drawn into their circle. When music started up out in the beer garden she went along quite happily as the rest of them swept outside.

Hips swinging in time to the music, cold beer in hand, she glanced around the bar, a dreamy, happy smile on her face. Despite her initial nervousness, she'd held her own with Lexie and Ross's loud, friendly group. No, more than held her own—she was having a good time. A great time. For the first time in her life there wasn't someone watching, waiting to remind her of what she should say or do or how her actions might be perceived. She wasn't worried about what Martin might think or living up to her grandparents' expectations.

She was on her own. Free. For the moment, anyway.

Which was when she glanced across the garden and locked eyes with Nathan Jones, leaning against the far wall with a beer in his hand as he watched her with a small, speculative smile.

3

NATE STARED ACROSS the sea of people at the woman in the
bright, breezy dress. It was amazing the difference a few hours
and, he guessed, a few beers could make. Gone was the pale,
tense society princess he'd met this afternoon and in her place
was a flush-faced blonde with a swing in her hips and a smile
on her lips. He almost hadn't recognized her, but nothing could
disguise the way she held herself and the tilt of her chin.

His gaze ran over her body again. Her red-and-yellow dress
ended just above the knees and tied around her neck. The
neckline was modest by island standards—half the girls in
the pub had come straight from the beach and there were
dozens of bikini tops and skimpy tank tops on display—but
it was tight and low enough to reveal that Elizabeth Mason
had great breasts.

He lifted his beer and took a long swallow, not taking his
eyes from her the whole time. The smile faded from her face
as their gazes connected, but she didn't look away, either, even
though he was pretty damn sure she wanted to.

He wasn't sure what was going on. He'd noticed her sexually this morning, there was no denying that—the shape of
her ass, the flash of her bra, the long line of her neck. But
she wasn't the kind of woman he'd been spending time with

lately—"spending time" being shorthand for casual sex, which was all he was good for these days. Elizabeth Mason had hard work written all over her. And that was before he even got into the whole mess of her being here to find her father.

And yet for some reason that he couldn't explain, he couldn't take his eyes off her.

Across the room, she finally looked away, turning her shoulder.

Against his smarter instincts, he pushed away from the wall and made his way toward her. He told himself every step of the way to rethink, to turn around and find some other woman to dance and drink and maybe go home with, but he didn't stop until he was standing behind her. Elizabeth must have sensed his approach because she tensed, the exposed muscles of her back flexing as though she was bracing herself.

"I figured you had to be around somewhere when Tania told me someone had tried to order a Pimm's," he said.

She didn't turn around, didn't so much as twitch.

He smiled. He hadn't been given the silent treatment since third grade. It hadn't worked then, either. He never had been able to resist a challenge.

He leaned a little closer, whispering right into her ear. "Do you want me to go away, Betty?"

"What do you think?" she said without moving.

He was standing so close he could see the fine blond hairs on the nape of her neck.

"I think that that was a pretty long look you gave me just now."

She swung to face him, ready to object. Her eyes widened when she registered his proximity. She took a quick step backward and crossed her arms protectively over her chest.

"Scared of me, Betty?" he asked, amused by how skittish she was.

"Of course not. And my name is Elizabeth, if you don't mind."

He cocked his head to one side. Was it his imagination, or did her accent get even snootier?

"Elizabeth is kind of an uptight name, don't you think? Makes me think of old ladies with scepters in their hands and cast-iron underwear."

"It's a very old, very traditional name, and it happens to be the one my parents gave me."

"Like I said, uptight."

Her nostrils flared. His smile widened into a grin. She was so prim, so proper—and so damned easy to get a rise out of. He hadn't had this much fun in a long time.

"What exactly is it that you want, Mr. Jones?"

He took a mouthful of beer and let his gaze slide past her chin to the neckline of her dress. Her perfume drifted toward him, something light and crisp and citrusy.

"Just being friendly. Making sure you settled in okay," he said.

She gave him a cool look. "Perhaps you could clarify something for me. Am I supposed to be charmed by all this? The smiles and the suggestive comments and the standing too close?"

"What do you think?"

"You don't want to know what I think, let me assure you."

"I can handle it, Betty, I promise. Hit me with your best shot."

She peered down her nose at him—quite the accomplishment given their difference in height. "My grandmother taught me that if you can't say something nice about someone, you shouldn't say anything at all."

"Your grandmother. That explains a lot."

Her eyes narrowed. "All right, then, since you insist, here

is what I think—that you believe an overdeveloped beefcake body and passable good looks give you a free pass to get away with anything where women are concerned."

He laughed. Couldn't help himself. "Overdeveloped? Which parts of me are overdeveloped?"

He watched, fascinated, as she blushed again.

"You have the fairest skin I've ever seen," he murmured. Every other body in the bar was brown from the Australian sun, but she was as pure and cool as a lily. He reached out a hand and ran his thumb along the curve of her cheekbone. As he'd suspected, she was as soft and smooth as silk.

She swallowed audibly. "Do you mind?" Her eyes were very wide, the pupils dilated.

"You know, I think I might, Betty," he said, surprising himself.

He dropped his hand. He'd crossed the bar to tease her, to fill in some time, to amuse himself on the way to oblivion. But she wasn't amusing. She was...disturbing, with her crisp, standoffish accent and tilted chin and uncertain eyes. For a moment they were both silent as they stared at each other.

"I'm not going to sleep with you, Mr. Jones."

That made him smile again. "No one asked you to, Betty."

Then, because she was too complicated, too messy, too challenging, he lifted his glass.

"Cheers," he said. He turned and walked away before she could say another word.

HE WAS UNBELIEVABLE. Earlier today she'd thought he was surly and uncooperative and rude, but now she added insufferably conceited and arrogant to the list of Nathan Jones's crimes. She honestly didn't know where he got off, touching her like that, standing so close she could smell the detergent he'd washed his clothes in and the sun-warmed, salty scent of his skin.

As for how he'd laughed at her and looked at her as though he could see straight through her clothes...

She'd never dealt with a man like him before. Cocky and arrogant and so...*physical* it was impossible to look at him and not imagine him on top of her, his heavy weight pinning her to the—

Elizabeth took a huge swallow of her beer. Why was it that when she thought about Nathan Jones her mind automatically descended below the waist?

She peeked out of the corners of her eyes to make sure that he really had disappeared into the crowd. He had and she relaxed a notch. With a bit of luck he'd leave the bar altogether and she wouldn't have to deal with him again.

A vain hope. Half an hour later she glanced across to where a few people had cleared some tables to create an impromptu dance floor to see Nathan in the middle of the swaying crowd, his arms around a small redheaded woman. The other woman was wearing a skimpy sundress with lots of strategic rips and tears in it, her swimsuit clearly visible underneath.

In London she'd be arrested for indecent exposure. At least Elizabeth hoped she would.

She watched as the woman wriggled in Nathan's arms, laughing into his face, one hand pressed flat against his chest. Nathan said something, then lifted his head suddenly and stared directly across the room at Elizabeth. She tensed as she met his pale blue eyes. She should have looked away before he caught her watching him. She should look away *now*.

Right now, before he got the wrong idea.

He lifted an eyebrow. Then the corner of his mouth curled up.

Smug bastard.

She tore her gaze away.

She could imagine what he was thinking—that the *uptight* English woman had the hots for him.

As if she'd be foolish enough to take up with a man like him, a man who was interested in nothing but sex. A man who wanted nothing but to get her naked and take his pleasure. A man who probably knew every sexual trick in the book and then some.

A wave of heat rolled over her.

Be honest with yourself at least, Elizabeth Jane. He fascinates you. You look at him and see every fantasy you ever had, every dirty thought you never dared share with anyone, including Martin.

It was true. It made self-conscious, nervous sweat prickle under her arms to admit it to herself, but it was true. She found Nathan Jones sexually attractive. Extremely sexually attractive.

How galling.

She turned and grabbed the nearby jug of beer and poured herself another glass.

He'd been so cocksure when he'd swaggered over to talk to her earlier. So confident of his reception. And she'd been so firm in her rejection. And all along he'd known. The look they'd just shared told her so.

He knew she'd been struck speechless by her first sight of him in all his bare-chested glory. He knew how images of his big body had been slipping into her mind against her will all day. How hot and sticky she felt just thinking about touching his firm, brown skin.

"Bloody hell," she whispered under her breath.

She felt as though she was on fire, could feel the echo of her heartbeat in the warm heat between her legs. She pressed her beer glass against her cheek, trying to cool down.

Crazy. This was crazy. She'd never felt so overheated and

overwrought in all her life. It must be the beer. Had to be. Otherwise—

A hand curled around her forearm and tugged her toward the dance floor.

"Come on, Betty, let your hair down," a voice murmured. "Dance with me."

She looked up into Nathan's lazy, heavy-lidded eyes. God, he was gorgeous. All angled cheekbones and straight nose and firm, chiseled lips.

She dug her heels in and shook her head as he pulled her another step closer to the dance floor.

"I don't want to dance. Not with you."

It was a lie, but it was also the truth. He terrified her. He made her scared of herself.

She tugged on her arm. He didn't let her go.

"Are you married?" he asked.

"No." Almost, but not quite.

"In a relationship?"

"No." Not anymore.

"Then what's the problem?"

He made it sound so simple, as though there were no other considerations apart from what she wanted and what he wanted right now. No tomorrow. No responsibilities or obligations or expectations.

When she didn't say anything she felt the grip on her arm loosen.

"Your call, Betty."

It should have annoyed her, the way he kept using that stupid diminutive of her name and the way he gave her a small, regretful smile and walked away again.

It didn't. Instead she was gripped with a sort of panicky, pressured fear that she'd just let an amazing opportunity slip through her fingers. When would she ever meet a man like him again? A feckless, pointless, incredibly sexy Lothario with nothing but pleasure on his mind? When would she ever be so far from home, so anonymous and free?

Because she didn't know the answers to any of those questions she pretended to herself that she'd narrowly escaped making a reckless, foolish decision and tried to look as though she was having a great time.

She watched him laugh and dance with another girl. Then another. She drank more beer and let her gaze run over his big, strong body as he moved on the dance floor or leaned against the far wall or stood in a loose circle with a bunch of surfer types, talking and laughing. She thought about the look in his eyes, remembered the way he'd touched her cheek. She thought about home, and how her grandparents had lied to her—with the best of intentions, yes, but it had still been a lie—and the way Martin touched her as though she were made of spun sugar and all the times she'd bitten her tongue and done the right thing and been a good girl, over and over again.

She thought about that moment in Harrods when she'd fantasized about destroying all that polished, expensive perfection.

I want him, a little voice whispered in her mind. *Why can't I have him?*

There were reasons—of course there were reasons—but they weren't good enough. They were safe and conservative and controlled and she was *so sick* of all those things. She wanted the unknown. Just this once. No one would ever know about it. It would be her secret, her moment of madness. A moment just for her, about her, about what she wanted, with no one else's feelings or opinions or judgments coming into play.

She put down her glass. Then she lifted her hands and checked to see that her hair was neatly pinned. Although why that should matter when she was about to proposition a man for the first time in her life, she had no idea.

She took a deep breath, then started across the room. She'd barely taken two steps before Nathan turned away from his friends and started weaving his way through the crowd toward the exit.

A surge of dismay rushed through her. He was leaving! Surely not, not when she'd just mustered the courage to ask for what she wanted. She paused for a split second, then she started pushing her way through the crowd, her movements increasingly urgent.

If he left without her saying what she wanted to say, doing what she wanted to do, she might never find the courage of this moment again.

She kept her eyes glued to Nathan's dark head and when he disappeared into the hallway leading to the front entrance she darted urgently past the last few people and was almost running when she entered the hallway.

It was empty. He'd already left.

Again, she hesitated. She couldn't very well chase him up the street. Could she? He'd issued his invitation, she'd rejected it. It was over. She'd missed her chance.

The disappointment and frustration she felt was so great that she was pushing through the double doors and out into the warm night before she could really consider what she was doing. There was no sign of Nathan on the street in either direction. Then she looked across the road toward the beach and saw a dark figure walking down the path toward the sand.

She crossed the road and strode to the top of the path. The moon was covered by clouds and the beach was dark, the water a glinting inky blackness in the distance. She set one foot on the sandy path, then stopped.

What was she doing, racing after a virtual stranger because he'd looked at her a certain way and said certain things? He was obviously going home for the evening. Whatever fleeting notion he'd had where she was concerned was long gone. She needed to turn around and go back to her room before this became embarrassing.

She turned away.

"Betty?"

She glanced over her shoulder. She could see Nathan silhouetted at the bottom of the path, a tall, broad shape.

Her heart kicked against her chest. She wiped her damp palms down the sides of her skirt. Then she walked down the path, into the darkness.

She stopped when she was standing in front of him. They were both silent for a beat.

"Were you going home?" she asked when the silence became excruciating.

"Getting some fresh air. Pretty warm in there."

Which meant she'd chased him out here like some sort of teenage desperado for nothing.

"I just thought… You asked me to dance before," she said lamely. "Maybe when you come back in we could…?"

His eyes glinted in the dim light. "You want to dance, Betty?"

She felt incredibly foolish and transparent. This was too, too humiliating. There was a reason why her first instinct had been to shy away from having anything to do with this man and this situation. She'd never done anything like this in her life before and she had no idea how to handle herself or him. For all she knew, she'd misread everything entirely and he really had been simply asking her to dance before.

"It doesn't matter," she said.

She turned away but his warm hand slid down her forearm and circled her wrist, stopping her from leaving.

"Come here," he said, very softly.

He tugged her gently toward him. For a moment she

resisted, her last doubts digging their heels in. Then his other hand slid around to cup the nape of her neck and she lifted her face as his head lowered toward her.

His lips were very soft as they found hers. She was surprised by how gentle he was, how sweet he tasted. His tongue flicked along the closed seam of her mouth, demanding entrance, and she found herself opening to him. And then he was inside her mouth, stroking, tasting, teasing. Sensation swamped her—her breasts flattened against his chest, the hard muscles of his arms pulling her closer, the avid hunger of his mouth. She made a needy sound and he pushed her head back farther as he delved more deeply, more greedily.

His hand left her nape to slide down her neck, across her shoulder and onto her breast. Liquid heat surged between her legs. She was so turned on it almost hurt. She pressed her knees together and dug her hands into the strong muscles of his shoulders and matched him kiss for kiss.

His thumb grazed her nipple through the fabric of her dress, then his warm hand slid beneath the halter top, making her gasp as he pinched and rolled her nipple between his fingers.

She had never felt like this in her life. So hot. So wet. So damned desperate to have a man's weight on top of her, inside her.

Nathan pressed his hips against her and she felt his erection against her belly. She slid a hand between them and traced him through the soft fabric of his well-worn jeans. So big, so thick.

He muttered something against her lips, then he ducked his head and kissed and licked a trail down her chest into her cleavage. He turned his head and sucked her nipple into his mouth, fabric and all, as both his hands found her ass. He squeezed her, hauling her closer, rubbing himself against her. His fingers curved beneath her butt cheeks, delving into the dark warmth between her legs. Teasing. Taunting. She shuddered and groaned.

"Please," she groaned, her head dropping back. "Please."

He lifted his head from her breasts and she heard him pull in a ragged breath. "Come on, Betty," he said, taking her hand.

He led her down to the beach. Her feet sank into the sand, and grit slipped between her feet and her sandals. She struggled to keep up with his long, urgent stride as he drew her away from the bright lights of Main Street and into darkness.

When the lights were a distant glow, he stopped and pulled her close again.

"Betty." He kissed her, and she could feel the smile on his lips.

Probably she should correct him—her name was Elizabeth, after all, and it looked as though they were about to have sex. But she didn't care. All her thoughts, all her focus were on one thing—the needy, desperate throb between her legs.

She slid her hands down the muscles of his belly to the waistband of his jeans. He wasn't wearing a belt and the denim gave easily as she tugged at one stud, then another, then another. She slid her hand inside his jeans and found the heat and hardness of him. She wrapped her fingers around him and stroked.

He started kissing her neck and she felt a tug behind her neck, closely followed by the coolness of the night air on her bare breasts as the untied halter of her dress dropped to her waist. He made an approving sound and cupped her breasts in both hands, his thumbs grazing her nipples over and over.

She started pulling at the waistband of his jeans, peeling them down over his hips.

"Easy, Betty," he whispered against her skin. "Easy."

"I want you," she said, the boldest words she'd ever spoken. "Inside me. Now."

He squeezed her breasts tightly in response. "What the lady wants."

As one they sank onto the sand, she on her back, him on top. Elizabeth opened her thighs and welcomed his weight as he pressed over her. He lowered his head and sucked first one nipple, then the other into his mouth. She arched her back and cried out. She was so close, so close. He hadn't even taken her panties off yet and already this was the most fulfilling, exciting sex of her life.

His hand skimmed up the inside of one of her widespread thighs and she gave an excited little gasp as his fingers found the damp silk of her underwear.

"Mmm," he said against her breast, clearly savoring her arousal. He stroked her through the damp silk before slipping his fingers beneath it to slide into her slick heat.

She closed her eyes and started to pant. His erection pulsed in her hand and she stroked her hand up and down more urgently, feeling the gentle velvet of the head, the silky steel of the shaft, the soft springiness of his hair.

He thrust a finger inside her. She bit her lip and lifted her hips, wanting more. A second finger slid inside her. She started to circle her hips.

So good. So good.

He pulled away from her for a moment and she felt him tugging at his jeans. She lifted her hips and pulled her panties down her legs, tossing them heedlessly to one side. She heard the faint crinkle of a foil packet and barely had time to register that he was using a condom before his weight was on her again and she was rising up to meet his penetration.

He slid inside her in one slick, powerful thrust, stretching her to the point of almost-pain. She sucked in a breath, her fingers clenching into his shoulders. She sucked in another as he started to move, pumping in and out of her, hot and hard and so good she couldn't believe it. His mouth was on her breasts, biting and licking and sucking her nipples. She slid her hands down onto the round, firm muscles of his backside and held on for dear life.

This was what she'd wanted. Mindless need. Heat. Slick wetness. This pressure building inside her. This wildness.

She could feel her orgasm approaching. She both craved it and feared it. She didn't want this to end. This was all her fantasies rolled into one, everything she'd ever dreamed about in the dark quiet of her bedroom while she pleasured herself with her own hands—no gentle words and respectful, considerate, careful caresses, just his hard body slamming into hers, the suck of his mouth on her breasts, the rasp of his hairy, hard body against hers, the rise of her hips to meet his, her hands, urgent and demanding on his body. This was almost everything she'd ever wanted, except—

"Could we... Could you... Do you think we could do it on our knees. With you behind me?" she asked.

He stilled. For a moment she thought she'd ruined everything. Martin had been appalled when she'd asked him to take her from behind. As sexual fantasies went, she hadn't thought it was too outrageous, but maybe nice girls didn't ask to do it doggy style. There were so many things she didn't know, after all. So many things she hadn't done.

Then Nathan withdrew from her and his hands found her hips. Excitement throbbed deep inside her as she followed his urging to roll over, rising up onto her knees almost immediately. He flipped her skirt up and out of the way and instinctively she arched her back, offering herself flagrantly. He muttered something under his breath. She felt the probe of his cock at her entrance, then he was sliding inside her, deeper than ever, filling her utterly.

"Oh. Yes! *Yes!*" she breathed.

It was better than she'd ever imagined. So deep. So full.

He started to move, stroking in and out of her. She heard

the slap of his thighs against her own, felt the rasp of his skin against hers. Heat rolled through her in waves, pushing her higher and higher. He reached a hand around her torso to tease her nipples. She started to gasp, pressing back against him urgently, tilting her hips and clenching her inner muscles.

So close, so close.

His hand slid down her belly and into the wet curls at the apex of her thighs. Then his fingers were teasing her in divine counterpoint to his thrusts, and she was done for.

Her orgasm hit her like a wall, rolling through her body, tensing her muscles, arching her back. She hissed between her teeth, groaned his name. And still it kept coming, pulsing, wet, mind-blowing. She felt him shudder, felt him push himself inside her with a new urgency, and then he was buried inside her, his body hard as granite against hers as he shuddered through his own climax.

There was a small silence afterward, a moment of absolute stillness, then he withdrew from her. She let her head drop forward, resting it on her fisted hands.

Her belly muscles were still trembling with the aftermath of her orgasm. Her legs felt weak. She even felt a little dizzy, as though all her blood had rushed south to the party and left precious little to spare for her brain.

"I thought Englishwomen were supposed to be uptight," Nathan said, his voice deep and amused.

"So did I."

She started to laugh. She felt amazing. Released. Relaxed. Revealed.

Right at that moment, nothing else mattered. Not the fact that they hardly knew each other, or that she was thousands of miles from home, or that she had no idea what to do next. There was only right here and right now. And it was damned good.

4

NATHAN WOKE IN A TANGLE of sandy limbs. He pushed a strand of pale blond hair off his face and blinked in the early morning light. For the first time in a long time his first thoughts weren't of Olivia. The reason for that was curled up against him on his bed, her backside snugged into the cradle of his hips, one of his arms draped around her body, his hand resting possessively on her breast.

Elizabeth Mason. Sam's daughter. The not-so-uptight English princess.

He was already half-hard, but he grew to full hardness as memories from last night came flooding back. Her hands down his jeans on the beach. The first slide of his fingers into her slick, ready heat. The way she'd begged him to take her from behind and then offered herself to him so eagerly. Her fervent, needy, lusty response to his every lick, suck, stroke or caress. They'd had sex again when they got back to his place, her on top this time, her cries ringing out into the night.

Not-so-uptight, indeed.

She stirred, her backside nudging against his stiff cock. He pressed a kiss to the nape of her neck, then nipped her skin gently. She tensed in his arms, fully awake.

Good.

He found her nipple with his thumb while he teased the sensitive skin of her nape with his tongue. Her nipples grew hard and she stirred again in his arms.

He eased her knee forward with his and reached behind himself to the bedside stand. Fifteen seconds later, he had a condom on and was pressing into her hot folds. She made an approving sound in the back of her throat as he slid inside her, the tight clench of her muscles closing around him.

She was incredible, so smooth and sweet-smelling and tight and wet. He rocked his hips, nudging just the head of his cock in and out, in and out. She moaned and he felt her inner muscles clutching around him. He'd meant to take it nice and slow—lazy, half-asleep morning sex—but she started to push against him and things quickly got urgent and sweaty and greedy. He grasped her hips and she rolled fully onto her belly, then up onto her knees.

He could feel how much she loved it like this, how much it excited her, which only made him harder and hotter. Then she arched her back and clenched her hands into the sheets as she came. He could feel her pulsing around him. Her inarticulate little sounds pushed him over the edge. He bent over her, panting his climax into her shoulder as he lost himself for a few precious seconds.

The ultimate forgetting. If only it lasted longer.

She collapsed on her belly afterward. He rolled to one side and took care of the condom. Then he flopped onto his back and for a moment they were both silent, the only sound their heavy breathing and the faint sound of the wind in the old liquid amber tree outside. The studio smelled of sex and clean sweat and her perfume and he let his gaze play over the perfect, fair skin of her back and her rounded, sweet-shaped behind.

That ass… That ass made him want to do a million bad, dirty things all at once.

"What time is it?" Her voice sounded husky and a little uncertain.

"Nearly seven."

She braced her elbows on the bed and propped her forehead on her hands. After a long moment she shifted her head slightly so she could see him out of the corners of her eyes. He raised an eyebrow when their gazes met.

She looked deeply uncertain and more than a little embarrassed. Maybe his first assessment hadn't been that far off. Maybe she was a little uptight, after all.

"Good morning," she said. She sounded very stiff, as though she'd rehearsed those two words several times in her mind before uttering them.

"Pretty good way to start it, anyway."

She rolled onto her back, carefully keeping the sheet over her breasts. Which struck him as being pretty amusing, considering he'd been inside her only a few minutes ago.

Her gaze slid toward the door and she frowned. He followed her eye line—her dress was crumpled on the floor just inside the doorway, a pool of red and yellow, her sandals kicked to one side.

He had a fair idea what she was frowning over, and his suspicions were confirmed when she reached for the T-shirt trailing off the end of the bed. He watched as she shrugged into it under the covers before sliding out of bed and collecting her dress. Her back turned, she stepped into the dress and didn't abandon his T-shirt until she was decently covered. He didn't have the heart to tell her that her skirt was caught up at the back, exposing the back of one lovely thigh and half a rounded butt cheek. She'd feel the breeze once she stepped outside, he figured.

She pulled her hair into a ponytail, plaiting it and then tucking it in on itself until it formed a loose knot on the back of her head. She had slender, graceful arms and hands, like a dancer's. He liked watching her move, even if her misplaced modesty was pretty damn funny.

He'd been so busy being entertained, it wasn't until she started to toe on her sandals that he realized she was about to race out the door.

While he hadn't exactly been a hound dog over the past few months, he hadn't lived like a monk, either, and he'd dealt with more than his fair share of morning-after coy looks and questions hinting at one night becoming more.

Clearly, there would be no such issues with his cool English lover.

"Is there a shoe sale on in town I don't know about?" he asked.

He ought to be grateful she was making it so clean and easy, but for some reason her eagerness to bail offended him. Not that he wanted her clinging to his chest and begging for a lifelong commitment, God forbid. But a little show of reluctance to draw a line under some of the best sex of his adult life might not go astray.

"I beg your pardon?"

He shrugged, not about to explain. If she wanted to go, she should go. He wasn't about to beg her to hang around.

He pushed back the covers and stood. She made a small, breathless sound as her gaze slid over his body. The hot, sticky look in her eyes went a long way to assuaging his ego. If he wanted to, he could have her in bed again within seconds.

The thought had barely registered before she reached for the door handle.

"I really have to go," she said.

Then, before he could open his mouth to respond, she was gone.

He blinked. Bloody hell. Talk about wham, bam, thank you, Nate. He'd never seen a woman so keen to get the hell out of Dodge before.

He shook off his irritation as he reached for a pair of cargo pants. So what? They'd had sex, it had been good, she'd bailed. Big deal. He probably wouldn't remember her name by the end of the week. Which was just the way he wanted it. No strings, no obligations, no guilt.

No possible way he could ever let anyone down ever again.

Pushing her from his mind, he went to make himself breakfast for one.

ELIZABETH REMEMBERED ENOUGH about the walk to Nate's place the previous evening to find her way back to the beach. From there it was a simple matter of turning her left shoulder to the water and walking until she hit the pier and the point where Main Street met the beach—except for the fact that with every step she was painfully aware of the fact that she was wearing no underwear. And that parts of her were feeling more than a little tender after three bouts of very active, very hot, very urgent sex with a man who gave absolutely no quarter in the bedroom.

She was such a hussy!

The way she'd chased after him. The way she'd propositioned him. The way—she pressed her hands over her face as the memory rushed up at her—the way she'd begged him to do her from behind.

She was shameless. Utterly shameless.

And the worst thing was, she didn't have it in her to regret any of it. It had been wonderful. She'd felt so free, so alive. And he'd been so amazing—generous and passionate and intuitive. He hadn't questioned anything, or made her feel silly or dirty or wrong, he'd simply thrown himself wholeheartedly into the moment. Just thinking about it made her want to—

She gave a shriek as an offshore breeze danced around her legs and her skirt kicked upward. She clamped her hands down on either side of her skirt. There was an older woman walking her dog down by the tide line and two joggers pounding the sand. She was sure they had all taken one look at her smudged makeup and mussed hair and understood that she'd just crawled out of bed. She didn't need to expose her naked nether regions to them to confirm the fact.

Which brought her to an important point she could no longer avoid: she had no idea where her panties were. The last time she could remember wearing them had been when Nathan had led her along the beach to find some privacy. She couldn't remember if she'd put them back on again for the walk to his place or not. She'd been so blown away after what had happened, so enamored of him, it was impossible to remember clearly.

A horrible thought hit her. What if she'd left them on the beach? The thought of her abandoned knickers being discovered by someone was enough to make her feel distinctly queasy. So very, very refined. If Grandmama could see her now...

Elizabeth pushed the thought away. She refused to feel guilty about last night. Yes, she'd had sex with an almost-stranger. The first one-night stand of her life. But it had been wild and sexy and sensual and she *would not regret it*. It was her private business and no one need ever know about it. What happened on Phillip Island stayed on Phillip Island.

Still, she kept an eye out for her knickers all the way back to the pub. She even backtracked a little, exploring the dry sand past the high-tide mark. She found nothing. She told herself that most likely they'd been swept out to sea and very badly wanted to believe it.

No one was stirring inside and she slunk up to her room gratefully. It was one thing to be determined not to feel regret and another thing entirely to do the walk of shame.

She showered and fell into bed for another couple of hours,

waking when the temperature began to climb again and the room became too stuffy for comfort. Sitting up in bed, she crossed her legs and pushed her hair back from her face and made some decisions.

Nate had offered to put her in contact with her father, even if it wasn't exactly in the manner of her choosing. She would wait until he heard something, then she would make her decision. There was nothing for her to rush home to, after all. She'd been working as a substitute teacher all year and the term was already over for her. Workwise, she could extend her stay in Australia until at least mid-January if she had to.

And—coward though it made her—maybe it would be better for herself and her grandparents to have a little breathing room before they came face-to-face again. Give tempers and ruffled feathers a chance to calm down.

And in the meantime, she would stretch her wings a little. Explore Cowes and the nearby beaches, get to know the locals a little. Find out what it was that Elizabeth Mason wanted in life if it wasn't marriage to a perfectly nice, perfectly perfect Englishman.

That ought to be enough to fill up her days. As for the nights...

A dozen hot and sweaty memories flitted across her mind. She pushed them away. Best not to think about the nights. She might be woefully naive in the world of casual sex, but she knew that looking for anything more than one night from a man like Nate was the emotional equivalent of playing Russian roulette.

She might have had a reckless moment, but she wasn't a reckless person.

NATE ARRIVED AT THE PUB shortly after six. The surf had been going off out at Kitty Miller Bay in the morning and he'd caught a lift out there with Tommy, then mowed the yard in the early afternoon. When he'd finished, he'd strung the old hammock between the studio and the liquid amber tree and sucked down a few beers in the drowsy afternoon heat.

Not a bad way to spend a day. If only he could stop his brain from thinking. Five minutes on his own without distraction and Olivia was there, filling his mind, tightening his gut, making him want to tear the world apart.

When beer alone didn't work its usual magic, he'd showered and pulled on a pair of jeans and a clean T-shirt and walked to the pub. There was more beer to be had there, of course—but the real lure was Elizabeth Mason. She of the sweet behind and soft, lily-white skin. In all the weeks he'd been holed up on the island, she was the first person or thing that had successfully distracted him from the mess in his own head long enough to offer any relief. He wasn't sure what it was that fascinated him so much. The apparent contradiction between her prim, conservative demeanor and the way she'd moaned in his arms? Her clipped British accent? The flashes of vulnerability and uncertainty he saw in her eyes?

She was a mystery. Perhaps that was all it was. An unknown quantity, an exotic, pale, well-spoken stranger in a world of nut-brown bodies, flat vowels, and sun and surf. Whatever. The important thing was that when he was with her he wasn't thinking about anything or anyone else.

She was sitting in the far corner with her English friends from the previous night when he entered the bar. She had her hair up again, neatly bound as though she was about to take dictation or chair a charity meeting. She was sitting straight, her posture perfect, with not even an elbow resting on the table. He smiled to himself as he ordered a beer. He bet she never slouched. Probably never swore, either, or jaywalked, or ate dessert before finishing her vegetables or cheated on her taxes.

Her head came up and her gaze searched the bar as if she

could feel him watching her. Their eyes met and locked. He reached into the front pocket of his jeans and tugged out a couple of inches of the scrap of pale blue silk and lace she'd left behind this morning. He raised his eyebrows in question.

"Yours?" he mouthed.

He had to bite back a laugh at her response. She jerked in her seat, then a rich tide of red rose up her chest and into her face. Her hands gripped the edge of the table, then she shot to her feet as though she was rocket propelled. He watched the bounce of her breasts as she marched toward him.

"You are disgusting," she said as she snatched her panties from his pocket and screwed them into a tight ball in her hand. "How dare you?"

He'd meant to tease her, but he could see that she was genuinely upset.

"Hey, Betty. Steady on," he said. He reached out to touch her arm but she jerked away from him.

Her hand was white-knuckle tight as she clenched it around her panties.

"I trusted you. Which makes me a fool, I see now. I thought last night was something private, between the two of us. How very naive and stupid of me."

"I'm sorry, okay? Don't get so hot under the collar. It was a joke."

"To you, perhaps. But now all the people in the bar know I slept with you last night. God only knows what they think of me."

Nate frowned. It had been a joke. A tease. No way had he expected her to react so strongly. Then he thought about her modesty this morning and realized that perhaps he should have. Clearly, she was a woman who worried about things like appearances and reputation. He bet himself a thousand bucks that she'd messed up her sheets this morning so that the hotel staff wouldn't guess she hadn't slept in her own bed. She'd probably been agonizing over where her panties were all day—then he'd walked in and teased her with his little show-and-tell routine.

"Relax, okay? Nobody saw, and nobody's thinking anything about you. They're all too busy getting pissed and trying to find someone of their own to shag to give two hoots about us."

She stared at him, her face stiff with tension. "What was I thinking? I must have been mad."

She said it so quietly he almost didn't hear her. Then she turned on her heel and pushed her way through the crowd until she reached the stairs. He watched her take them two at a time, her back stiff with tension.

"Shit." He took a mouthful of beer. Not in a million years had he meant to hurt her. He'd wanted to make her laugh, get that martial light in her eye, provoke her into insulting him some more in that hoity-toity way of hers.

He turned to face the bar, resting his elbow on the scarred wood. Next time he saw her, he'd apologize. Once she'd had a chance to calm down, she'd understand.

He tried to push the incident from his mind, but ten minutes later he glanced over and saw a waitress deliver a round of meals to the table where Elizabeth had been sitting. Her English friends looked confused and he could see them searching for Elizabeth as the waitress stood with an unclaimed burger and fries.

Great. She'd abandoned her dinner because of him.

Damn it.

He pushed his beer away and crossed the bar.

"Elizabeth wasn't feeling so great," he explained to her worried friends. He took the plate from the waitress. "Thanks, Sall. I'll take this up to her room for her."

"Sure. Thanks, Nate." Sally gave him a quick smile before heading back to the kitchen.

He left the table before Elizabeth's friends could ask any more questions, stopping by the bar for a quick detour before heading upstairs.

The barman had given him Elizabeth's room number and he balanced the plate on his raised knee as he knocked on her door.

There was a short pause before a voice answered.

"Who is it?"

"Room service."

Another pause. Then the door opened.

"I didn't— Oh. You."

Her face was still flushed and a few strands of hair had escaped from her neat hairdo.

"You forgot your burger." He lifted his other hand. "And I thought you might be thirsty."

Her gaze fell on the Pimm's and lemonade in his outstretched hand.

"I'm not hungry. Or thirsty."

He shouldered his way past her and put down the plate on the bedside table, placing the glass beside it.

"Better eat it quickly before it goes cold."

"I'm not hungry," she repeated. "And I'd very much appreciate it if you'd leave my room."

He studied her a moment, wondering how to get past her to-the-manor-born outrage. "Elizabeth. I'm sorry, okay? It was dumb. Really dumb. I was trying to be funny, not humiliate you. Okay?"

"Funny? Clearly your sense of humor and mine are vastly different, because making a public display of something that should be a very private matter is not my idea of amusing."

"Look, if I could take it back, I would. But I can't. And your burger is getting cold, and I don't want that on my conscience, as well."

She crossed her arms over her chest. "I'm not going to choke down food I don't want simply because you've suddenly developed a conscience."

She started to say more, but he reached down and grabbed a couple of fries and put them in her mouth.

She spluttered, but she was far too polite to spit them back out. He watched as she chewed furiously.

"You really are an absolute pig, aren't you?" she said once she'd swallowed.

"Maybe. Want some more?"

"No!" she said. Then her tongue darted out to lick a salt crystal from the corner of her mouth.

He laughed and she looked hugely chagrined. "Busted," he said. He offered her the plate again. "Going hungry isn't going to punish anyone except yourself."

"You think you're so clever and charming, don't you?" She snatched the plate from him.

She sat on the bed and rested the plate on her knees.

"Actually, no. I don't." He straddled the battered wooden chair by the window and rested his forearms on the back.

"Yes, you do. You think you're irresistible, but you're not. You didn't charm me just now, and you didn't charm me last night. I slept with you for my own reasons, not because of anything you did or said. And I'm eating my dinner because I paid for it and I'm hungry."

She picked up her burger and took a big, screw-you bite out of it.

"Whatever floats your boat, Betty."

She frowned at him ferociously until she'd swallowed and could speak again.

"Please stop calling me that. My name is Elizabeth."

"You're right. You're not really a Betty."

"Thank you."

"More of a Lizzy."

She sighed heavily, rolled her eyes and took another bite of her burger.

"Mind if I have one of your fries?" He didn't wait for her to respond, simply grabbed a handful.

"Have you ever seen the movie *Greystoke?*" she asked.

"I think so. That's the fancy Tarzan one, yeah? With Christopher Lambert? Why?"

"You put me in mind of a certain man who was raised by wild apes."

She looked pretty pleased with herself for getting a shot in, and he rewarded her with a laugh before helping himself to more fries.

"Nice one, Lizzy."

She tried not to smile, but her lips kept curling up at the corners.

"How's that burger?"

"Very nice. Thank you," she said grudgingly.

"I meant to tell you—I left a message with Sam today. Hopefully he'll get back to me soon."

"Oh. Can I ask what message you left?" She looked worried.

"If you're asking if I left a voice-mail message telling him about his long-lost, possibly unknown daughter, the answer is no. I simply told him he needed to call, stat."

"Well. Thank you."

"You're welcome. Are you going to eat the rest of that burger?"

"I suppose I should be grateful you didn't grab it from my hand," she said as she offered the plate to him.

She drank her Pimm's while he polished off the burger.

"I suppose you'd like me to leave you some of this, too?" she asked, arching an eyebrow in inquiry.

"Lizzy, I'm happy to say it's all yours. Foul stuff."

"Have you even tried it?"

"Yes. Once. Which was more than enough."

"It's very refreshing."

"Sure it is." He stood and dusted his hands down the front of his jeans.

She swallowed the last of her Pimm's, then stood, as well.

"We okay?" he asked.

She nodded briefly. Ever so gracious, as always. As always where she was concerned, he couldn't help smiling.

"At least wait until you've left before you laugh at me," she said primly.

"I wasn't laughing at you, Lizzy."

She walked past him and opened the door.

"Thank you for my dinner. And the apology."

He walked toward the door but stopped when he was in front of her.

"Don't I get a goodbye kiss?" he asked, his eyes on her full lower lip.

"I don't think that would be a very good idea, for a lot of reasons."

"So? It'd be fun, at the very least." He leaned toward her.

She put her hands on his chest. "Is fun all that you ever think about?"

An image of Olivia flashed across his mind. The blood on her face. Her fear-filled eyes.

"No," he said, then he closed the last, small distance between them and kissed her.

She tasted sweet and tangy from the Pimm's. He slid his hands over her shoulders and down her back to cup her ass. Her peachy, round ass. She made a low sound in the back of her throat. He stroked her tongue with his and pressed forward with his hips, instinctively seeking the heat and softness of her body. He was hard—had been half-hard the whole time he'd been in her room, simply from smelling her perfume and being close to her—and a small shudder of anticipation rolled through his body.

He slid one hand from her backside to smooth it up her ribcage to her breasts. Her nipples were already stiff, poking through the soft fabric of her sundress. He flicked one shoulder strap down, then the other, and her breasts were bare and he was filling his palm with warm, resilient flesh.

He plucked at her nipples, teased them, but he wanted to taste her, the way he had last night. He broke away from her mouth, kissing his way across her cheekbone, lingering at the soft skin below her ear, and continuing to her breasts. Her nipples were a pale shell-pink, small and pretty. He tongued first one, then the other. Elizabeth's hands slid into his hair, holding him against her breasts.

As if he wanted to be anywhere else.

He slid a hand down her thigh to the hem of her dress, sweeping beneath it. She spread her legs eagerly as his hand slid up her thigh and into wet heat. His cock ached as he remembered how tight she'd been last night, the fierce pull of her body on his.

He stroked her through the silk of her underwear and suddenly he couldn't wait a moment longer. One hand still on her mound, he lifted his head from her breasts and pushed her two steps backward until she was flattened against the wall. She watched him through heavy-lidded, smoky eyes as he fumbled at his waistband, dragging his fly down. He found a condom and slid it on with urgent hands. He was too impatient to wait for her to pull off her panties; he simply pushed them to one side, then he lifted her knee so it hooked over his hip and slid inside her.

She closed her eyes and moaned. Man, he loved the sounds she made, the little gasps and sighs.

He grasped her hips and started to move inside her. So tight. So hot. So damned good. He hitched her other leg up and she hooked her ankles together behind his back and thrust her hips forward to meet his strokes.

He could feel her excitement rising, the tension ratcheting tighter and tighter inside her. He lowered his head and licked her breasts, left, then right, pulling on her nipples until she gasped his name. Her fingers dug into his back and she held her breath, straining, almost there…then she pulsed around him, arching away from the wall.

He kissed her, swallowing her cry of release. He closed his eyes and concentrated on the slick heat encasing him, the warm brush of her breasts against his chest, the flex of her hips beneath his hands as she kept his rhythm.

There was nothing in the world except for her and him and the slide of their bodies and the sound of their breathing. Perfect peace. Absolute oblivion.

Too quickly his climax found him, tightening to a point of white heat and need until he pressed his face into her neck and thrust inside her one last time to shudder out his release.

He kept his face pressed into the soft skin of her neck for long moments afterward, regretting the loss of mindlessness, begrudging the return to reality.

Without releasing his grip on her hips, he pushed away from the wall and carried her to the bed. He stayed inside her as he lowered her onto the bed.

Then he started kissing her again, seeking that moment of peace once more.

5

ELIZABETH WOKE TO THE soft snick of the door closing. She opened her eyes and propped herself up on one elbow, disoriented in the dark of the room. For a moment she didn't know where she was—her bedroom in Mayfair, Martin's apartment, the hotel room in Soho. Then the languid heat between her legs and the slight soreness of her breasts brought it all rushing back: Nathan, his visit to her room, sex against the wall.

She was in Australia. And she'd just spent her second night in the arms of the sexiest man she'd ever met.

She thought about all the times she'd lain beneath Martin, yearning for something other than his gentle, careful lovemaking. She hadn't known what that something was until she'd found it on the beach and against the wall in her hotel room. She'd wanted passion. Desire. Animal lust. She'd wanted sweat and grabby hands and panting and undeniable need.

She rolled onto her side and stared at the crack of light seeping beneath the blind on the window.

A few days ago, she'd never had sex anywhere except in a bedroom. She'd never experienced any other position except missionary. She'd certainly never been slammed against a wall and had her lover so desperate to be inside her that he hadn't even bothered to remove her underwear.

It was just sex, of course. Bodies rubbing against each other because it stimulated nerve endings and satisfied some primal urge. But if she hadn't seen her birth certificate, if she hadn't confronted her grandfather, if she hadn't acknowledged almost too late that there were fundamental problems in her relationship with Martin and that she was shoehorning herself into a future that suited everyone except herself, she might have married him. She might have made her vows and settled into a life half-lived. She might have gone on denying herself and her needs and never known the joy, the freedom of being able to express her desires. Better yet, to pursue them.

So, yes, it was just sex, but at the same time it felt like much, much more than that. As though she was on an archeological dig, searching for herself, and her sexuality was the first truth that she'd uncovered.

Memories from the night washed over her as she lay drowsing. Nathan's body, so hard and strong beneath her hands. The firm, deeply satisfying thrust of him inside her. The way he'd barely let her catch her breath and come down to earth before he started kissing and touching and torturing her all over again. He was an insatiable lover. Driven. Intense. Almost desperate, it had seemed to her more than once during the night, like a drowning man clutching at passion and desire to keep him afloat. The look in his eyes, the fervor in his caresses…

Elizabeth let out a huff of laughter at her own melodrama. Nathan Jones was a surf bum with a fabulous body and a talent for sex. There was no need to read anything else into his admittedly intense lovemaking. In fact, there was no need to overanalyze it at all. It was meaningless and pleasurable and wonderful, and she was content to leave it that way.

A knock sounded at the door, drawing her out of her thoughts. Since she knew only a handful of people in all of

Australia and only one of them knew where she was staying, she thought it was safe to assume it was Nate.

A slow smile curled her mouth. She'd thought he'd gone home, but perhaps he'd simply ducked out to buy a bottle of water or make a call or buy a newspaper or something and now he was back to put in an encore performance.

Remembering the morning sex they'd enjoyed yesterday, she hoped so. She got out of bed and wrapped a towel around her torso and opened the door.

And promptly gaped.

Because standing there in a very wrinkled three-piece suit, overnight bag in one hand, briefcase in the other, was Martin.

"My God. What on earth are you doing here?" she said.

Not the most welcoming of greetings, but he was supposed to be in London.

"I came to talk to you. Since you didn't seem to want to talk over the phone."

"But…this is *Australia!*" she said, still not quite able to comprehend his presence.

"Yes, after nearly twenty-four hours in the air, I'm well aware of that. Might I come in?"

It was a perfectly reasonable request—if they were still engaged. But they weren't. And she'd spent the night having sex with another man in the rumpled sheets just over her shoulder. It felt hugely, hugely wrong to invite Martin into the same space that she'd recently shared with Nathan. Especially when she was only wearing a towel.

"Could you give me a moment to dress?"

She closed the door before he could answer, feeling both guilty and ungenerous as well as angry and ambushed.

There was only one person who could have told him where she was: Violet. For a moment she was seized with the urge to call her friend and blast her for first blabbing, then not making contact to warn Elizabeth that she'd blabbed. She sat on the room's one and only chair and closed her eyes.

Who was she kidding? She could work up a righteous head of anger at Violet for blabbing and Martin for ambushing her but the truth was that she was swamped with guilt. A week ago, the man on the other side of the door had had every reason to believe that he would be spending the rest of his life with her. She'd given him her virginity at the ripe old age of twenty-three after dating him for four months. Six months ago, he'd asked her to marry him and she'd said yes. They'd had an engagement party and booked the Savoy for their reception and St. Stephen's for the ceremony and Paris for the honeymoon. And then she'd pulled the rug out from under his feet and run away to the other side of the world before the dust had even settled.

She owed him a conversation. An explanation. The fact that he'd chosen loyalty to her grandfather over loyalty to her didn't change that or excuse her actions. Yes, she had been shocked. Resentful, too, although she wasn't sure that Martin was the right target for her resentment. But she'd had time to calm down now and they needed to talk.

She dressed quickly in one of her new sundresses and brushed out her hair before tying it back in a simple ponytail. She would have killed for a shower, but it was not to be, not when Martin was standing out in the hall like Paddington Bear, abandoned at the train station.

She straightened the bed, then let him into the room.

"It's a long flight. Would you like a shower?" she asked, gesturing toward the ensuite.

"Yes. That's probably a good idea. I suspect my personal hygiene leaves pretty much everything to be desired right now." He offered her the ghost of a smile. "I won't be long."

She handed him a fresh towel and sat on the bed to wait as he disappeared into the bathroom.

This was going to be difficult. There was no getting around it. Martin had not flown halfway around the world to find closure. He'd come to talk her into coming home and getting married. And she was going to say no, and he was going to be hurt all over again.

She stared at her lap. It wasn't as though she had a choice. She couldn't marry him simply to avoid hurting him. That would only hurt him far more in the long term, even if she was prepared to sacrifice her own happiness in the name of doing the right thing. And she wasn't. She'd put a lid on her own feelings, wants and needs for too long, first bowing dutifully to her grandparents' idea of who she should be, then to Martin's.

No longer.

The water shut off abruptly and she crossed to the corner counter and turned the kettle on. By the time Martin emerged from the bathroom in a fresh white shirt and a pair of slightly wrinkled, tailored trousers the tea was ready to pour.

She made him a cup the way he liked it and passed it over wordlessly. He took the lone chair and she returned to her spot on the edge of the bed.

Martin glanced around the room, taking in the dingy carpet and basic furnishings before focusing on her. She held his eye and took a deep breath.

"Martin, I don't want to hurt your feelings, but I'm not coming back to London with you."

"I understand that you're keen to meet your biological father—"

"It's not that. That's why I'm here, yes. But that's not why I can't go back with you. I'm incredibly sorry that it's taken all this to open my eyes, but I can't marry you."

Martin looked down at the mug of tea in his hands. "Can I ask…is there someone else?"

"No." Which was true. Her decision to call off the wedding

had come long before she even knew Nathan Jones even existed.

Martin drew breath to ask another question and she rushed into speech.

"I know you're confused. I know this must seem like it's come out of nowhere, but it hasn't. It's been building for years. Ever since I dropped out of field hockey when I was fifteen."

Martin shook his head. "Hockey. I'm afraid I must be incredibly dense, Elizabeth, but I'm struggling to see how your hockey team has anything to do with our relationship."

"My grandmother hated the idea of me playing. She thought it was rough and dangerous, but I adored it. Then Grandmama came to the semifinal and I got checked and fell over and she was so upset after the game that I promised to quit on the spot. And I've been doing it ever since, Martin. I dropped English Literature and took up Fine Arts as an elective and didn't accept a full-time teaching position when I graduated because she wanted me to take over her seat on the Friends of the Royal Academy Committee and the other charities she sits on. I didn't get my hair cut because my grandfather prefers it long. I didn't go backpacking through Europe with Violet because they were worried about my safety—"

"You're saying you feel an obligation to please them."

"That's it, exactly. I love them enormously, but the truth is I've let them dictate too many of my decisions. To the point where I don't even know what I want anymore."

"I understand what you're saying, but it won't be like that once we're married. You'll be in your own home, your choices will be your own to make. I certainly have no plans to impose my will on you."

"Martin—" She broke off, feeling incredibly sad as she looked at him. "Don't you see? You were their choice, too, in a way. Don't you remember how they sat us together at the firm Christmas party, and how my grandmother encouraged you to ask me to dance? And how my grandfather kept asking you to drop his papers by at the house when he 'forgot' to bring them home from the office so we'd keep running into each other?"

"Elizabeth, I can assure you that the only reason I have ever been interested in you is for yourself."

She could see the devotion in his eyes, the adoration—and she knew she was utterly unworthy of it. Not because she was a bad person, but because he had an idea in his head of who she was, and it had nothing to do with the real Elizabeth.

She searched her mind for a way to explain the fundamental disconnect between them.

"Remember that time I wanted to talk about our sex life?" she asked. "Remember how I asked you to, you know, do it differently, and you refused?"

"I remember Violet putting ideas in your head."

"Those were my ideas, Martin. I wanted you to do those things to me. But you said you respected me too much."

"You'd prefer for me to throw you over my shoulder or do you in the backseat of my car rather than taking the time to ensure your needs are met, would you?"

"Well, honestly, yes. Sometimes I would. Haven't *you* ever wanted to do any of those things?"

He broke eye contact and slid his mug onto the bedside table before smoothing his hands down his thighs. The very picture of discomfort.

"Of course I've wanted to do those things. There are lots of things I'd like to do, but that doesn't mean I'm going to cast all other considerations aside and jump in, boots and all. Life isn't only about what you want, Elizabeth."

Elizabeth put down her own mug of tea. "I'm going to take a guess that when it comes to me the 'other considerations' that come into play are my grandparents. Am I right or am I wrong?"

Martin threw his hands in the air. "Again with your grandparents. Could you please stop trying to equate their values with mine? I respect them enormously, especially your grandfather. He's a brilliant lawyer and he's been an incredibly generous mentor to me. I owe him everything. But I'd like to think I have enough native wit and intelligence to make my own decisions."

She stared at him, frustrated. How to get through to him?

"Look me in the eye and tell me that when I asked you to do me from behind like a dog you didn't once think of my grandfather and what he might think and how much you respect him," Elizabeth challenged boldly.

"For God's sake, Elizabeth. What a question." His color was high as he shifted in his chair.

"Okay, fine, answer me this, then—have you ever done it that way with one of your other girlfriends?"

She saw the truth in his eyes before he glanced away. She leaned forward to capture his hands, forcing him to return his focus to her.

"Let's call a spade a spade here. For better or for worse, I'm fixed in your mind as the granddaughter of the man you respect more than any other person in the world. You said it yourself—you owe him everything. When you look at me, you see the granddaughter of Edward Whittaker first and me second."

Martin reversed their grips so that he was the one holding her hands. "Elizabeth, I love you."

"Martin, the woman you think you want to marry doesn't exist. She's a construct, cobbled together by my overdeveloped sense of duty and your desire to be connected to a man who, in many respects, has filled the role of father in your life. I would make a terrible, terrible wife for you."

"I don't believe that. Not for a minute."

"It's true. You might not see it now, but you will one day."

He stared at her and she could see realization dawn on him as he at last understood that he would be going home alone.

"I'm so sorry. I really am. You're a good, good man. And one day you are going to make some woman an amazing, wonderful, loving husband. But that woman is not going to be me."

His eyes were suspiciously shiny. He stood, pulling his phone from his pocket.

At first she thought he was calling her grandparents, but then she realized he was talking to the airline, booking the next available flight to London. She put her hand on his arm to get his attention.

"Why don't you stay for a few days? You don't have to go straight back, do you?"

He covered the mouthpiece on his phone. "I didn't come here for a holiday. I came here for you."

So she sat with guilt gnawing at her while he booked a flight home for late that evening, reminding herself over and over that she'd done the right thing for both of them, that whatever hurt she inflicted now was better than a divorce down the road when things would be even more messy and complicated and painful.

It didn't make her feel much better.

Martin ended his call and reached for his overnight bag.

"Now what are you doing?" she asked.

"I need to get back to Melbourne."

"It's only an hour and a half away. You can at least stay for breakfast, can't you?"

He considered her invitation for a long moment. "I don't particularly relish being the object of your pity, Elizabeth."

"I don't pity you, Martin. How could I? You're one of the smartest, most honorable men I know. I feel bad about the way things have turned out. I wish I'd found the courage to stand up for myself before the business with the birth certificate. But I don't feel sorry for you. Somewhere out there is a woman you're going to want to throw over your shoulder, and nothing in the world is going to stop you from doing it. I look forward to hearing about her when it happens."

He stared hard at the floor for a few beats, then he put down his overnight bag.

"Where do you recommend for breakfast, then?"

NATE HITCHED A LIFT out to Woolamai in the morning. The swell was high and the water crowded with fellow surfers keen to take advantage. He spent an hour in the water, got sandbagged twice and relentlessly drilled when a wave shut down with him in the curl. His brain felt washed clean and he was starving by the time he hit the beach.

A couple of New Zealand surfers were heading into town and he caught a ride with them. He thought about Elizabeth as he sat in the back of their pickup. The silk of her skin. The taste of her. The smell of her hair.

He'd had her three times last night, and still he wanted her again. He wasn't sure what was up with that, but he wasn't going to question it. Far better to have his head filled with visions of soft white skin and pretty pink nipples and pale blond hair than what he'd been living with for the past few months.

He wondered if he'd see her again tonight. Then he smiled to himself. He'd make sure he did. Why leave it to chance, after all?

He spotted the thick white envelope sticking out of his

mailbox as he lifted his board off the New Zealanders' roof rack. His mood soured. Just what he needed—a reminder of everything he'd turned his back on.

He tugged the envelope free on his way past, not even glancing at the red-and-black logo in the top left corner. He dumped his board by the back door and threw the envelope into the corner of the kitchen as he entered. It slapped against the stack of other envelopes piled there, all of them unopened. One day soon he'd get around to dumping the lot of them in the recycle bin.

He took a quick shower, threw on fresh clothes, then did a lap of the house, trying to decide what to do next, feeling off-kilter thanks to that damn envelope. Pathetic that that was all it took these days.

Thoughts of Elizabeth flashed across his mind again, but he could hardly go looking for her so soon after leaving her bed. He needed to watch himself where she was concerned as it was.

He did another lap of the house, anxiety nipping at his ankles. He didn't do alone time without a beer in his hands and it was definitely too early to drink. Making a quick decision, he grabbed his wallet and walked out the door. He'd head into town, get something to eat, maybe grab some groceries for the next few days. That ought to kill an hour or two.

The first person he saw when he hit main street was Elizabeth, sitting at one of the tables on the sidewalk outside the Euphoria Cafe. All his self-strictures about being careful where she was concerned went out the window. She looked so soft and cool and he could practically feel her skin beneath his hands. He was about to cross to her table when a tall, dark-haired man exited the café and sat with her. There was something about the way the guy looked at her that got Nate's back up. The feeling only intensified when the guy picked up her hand and held it. And she let him. She even laughed at something he said and squeezed his fingers.

Elizabeth had told him she was single. She'd lain down on the beach with him and tangled his sheets and a few hours ago had taken him in her mouth and made him a little bit crazy. So who the hell was this guy? This pale, overdressed stiff with his ridiculous pants and business shirt and banker's haircut?

He was already striding toward their table when it hit him that his reaction was way over the top. Elizabeth owed him nothing. They'd slept with each other twice. They'd made no commitments to each other, tacit or overt.

So why the hell was he standing at her table, glaring down at her?

"Lizzy. Long time no see," he said.

Her eyes widened with shock. "Nathan. Hello. Um. Yes."

Nate could feel the other guy checking him out and he straightened to his full height. Hard to tell with the other man sitting down, but Nate figured he had a couple of inches on him. He met the other guy's eye and offered his hand.

"Nathan Jones."

"Martin St. Clair," the guy said, his accent a perfect match for Elizabeth's clipped tones.

"Nathan shares a house with my father. He's helping me make contact with him," Elizabeth explained. She flipped her teaspoon over and over nervously.

"I see. It's nice to know Elizabeth has friends to help her out when she's so far from home," St. Clair said.

It was such a pompous, stiff little speech that Nate couldn't help smirking. St. Clair didn't look much older than him—early thirties—so what was with the big stick up his ass?

"I'm more than happy to help Elizabeth out. In fact, it's been my pleasure," he said.

Elizabeth's eyes narrowed, even as her cheeks turned pink.

That was the problem with that creamy English complexion of hers—it was a dead giveaway every time.

St. Clair was looking back and forth between the two of them, a frown on his face.

"Have you known Blackwell long?" he asked.

"About ten years or so." Nate could elaborate, but he chose not to. Knowledge was power, after all.

He switched his attention to Elizabeth, who was positively glowering at him now.

"I'm free to talk about that thing again tonight, by the way," he said. "What time suits you?"

"I'll have to get back to you." Her accent even more cut-glass than usual.

He shrugged. Then, because he was far too aware of her English lover or whoever St. Clair was, Nate slid his hand onto the nape of her neck and ducked his head to kiss her goodbye. She tasted like coffee and she jerked her head backward when he slipped his tongue inside her mouth.

"Nice meeting you, Martin," Nathan said as he straightened.

He gave them both a finger wave before turning and sauntering up the street toward the bakery.

So much for his perfect distraction.

ELIZABETH FOUGHT THE URGE to squirm in her seat. There was no way that Martin had not picked up on the not-very-subtle signals Nathan had been sending. The man had practically cocked his leg, he'd marked his territory so obviously.

She could only imagine what Martin must be thinking. She snuck a look at him from beneath her lashes. He was studying a sugar sachet, smoothing his thumb back and forth over the small square.

She felt a strong urge to apologize, even though that would

only confirm that she'd slept with another man mere days after ending their engagement. She opened her mouth, but something stopped her from saying the words on the tip of her tongue. She remembered the strange, almost scary euphoria she'd felt after that first night with Nathan. The feeling of freedom.

And suddenly it hit her that she didn't owe Martin anything. Their relationship was over. Had been since the moment she'd called off the wedding in London. She hoped that they would remain friends, but she wasn't going to pretend to be something she wasn't to achieve that. If Martin chose to judge her, that was his decision, not hers. At the end of the day, the only person whose opinion she needed to worry about was her own.

It was a strange realization. A revolutionary concept. She'd lived for the good opinion of others for so long, it felt like shedding a huge weight. Just last night she'd been mortified because Nathan had teased her by displaying an inch of her underwear in the bar. She'd retreated to her room and imagined what judgments people must be making about her, what they must be whispering to each other. She was so used to living in the fishbowl of her grandparents' elite, discreet social circle that it simply hadn't occurred to her to not care what anyone else thought.

Because, really, it didn't matter that a few people she'd probably never see again might suspect she'd had sex with Nathan Jones. In the big scheme of things, it was neither here nor there. It was none of their business. Pure and simple. And if they chose to judge her, then so be it. She couldn't control how other people saw her. Which, essentially, was what she'd been trying to do all her adult life.

She met Martin's gaze across the table.

"Thank you for breakfast. I know you want to get back to

Melbourne, but you should at least come for a walk along the beach before you go."

He put the sugar sachet down and placed his palms flat on the table.

"Thank you, but no. I think I need to go home."

She nodded. She understood. And she regretted his pain. But she was not going to apologize. For perhaps the first time in her life. She owed herself—her new self—that, at least.

They both stood and walked to the pub to collect Martin's bags. Then she walked him to his rental car and watched as he stowed his luggage. When he was done, he turned to her and eyed her for a long, silent moment, his gaze roaming over her face.

"Look after yourself, Elizabeth."

"I will. You do the same, okay?"

She hesitated, then she stood on tiptoes and pressed a kiss to his cheek. His lashes swept down as he closed his eyes, then, as she was about to withdraw, his arms closed around her and he pulled her close in a fierce bear hug.

She hugged him back, thinking about the many hours they'd spent with each other, the many kindnesses he'd shown her. She loved him very much—as a friend. He was a lovely man. He simply wasn't the man for her.

His arms loosened and she took a step backward. He cleared his throat.

"Goodbye, Elizabeth."

She waited until his car had driven out of sight before marching down to the beach. What on earth had led Nathan to put on such an obvious display? Was it some kind of chest-beating alpha-male thing? Or was it yet another example of his warped sense of humor, more teasing in line with his stunt with her underwear?

Whatever it was, it was unacceptable. The sun was at its zenith, the sand hazy with heat as she walked along the high-tide mark and then up the short track to her father's street. She spotted Nathan the moment she rounded the corner of the house; he was lounging in a hammock strung between his studio and one of the lower branches of the big tree that shaded much of the backyard. His eyes were closed and he was nursing a bottle of beer against his bare chest.

As angry as she was with him, it was impossible not to appreciate the sheer physical beauty of the man. Shaking her head at herself, she strode up to the hammock and gave it a hard yank.

The hammock tilted dramatically, dumping Nathan unceremoniously facedown onto the grass.

He swore, his words muffled. Then he rolled onto his back and stared up at her, his chest glistening with spilled beer. "What was that for?"

"Take a wild guess."

He braced his arms on the ground and pushed himself to his feet. She tried not to notice the way his abdominal muscles flexed invitingly.

"What you did was incredibly inappropriate. Not to mention embarrassing," she said.

"I kissed a friend goodbye. Where's the harm in that?"

"That wasn't a kiss. That was a brand. You were marking your territory."

"Don't flatter yourself, sweetheart."

She crossed her arms over her chest. "What was it, then? Why did you kiss me like that in front of Martin?"

He shrugged a shoulder before bending down to collect his beer bottle.

"I don't know. It was just an impulse. A bit of fun. Unlike certain people, I don't spend half my life staring at my own navel, analyzing every thought and body function."

"Well, maybe you should. It might stop you from behaving like a fifteen-year-old boy half the time."

To her enormous chagrin, he laughed. "Lizzy, we really have to do something about your insults. That one couldn't fight its way out of a soggy paper bag."

She pointed a finger at him. "Don't attempt to disarm me with your cheap charmer's tricks. You wanted to embarrass me this morning. You might not want to admit it, but I know it and so do you."

"You're way too uptight, you know that?" He reached for her, trying to pull her close.

She slipped out of his grasp. "No. No more. Good sex is not an excuse for bad behavior. You might not respect me, but I do. Goodbye, Nathan."

She turned on her heel and started walking.

"Lizzy."

She turned the corner into the driveway. She told herself it was probably a good thing to draw a line under whatever it was that had been going on between her and Nathan. She wasn't in the market for a holiday fling. She wasn't in the market for anything. She was here seeking contact with her father, nothing more.

"Elizabeth."

His hand caught her shoulder as she was about to step onto the road. They faced each other under the bright midday sun.

"I'm sorry, okay? I saw you with that guy, the way he was looking at you, and you'd told me there was no one else, and...I don't know. It just pissed me off."

She stared at him. Was it her imagination, or was Nathan telling her that he'd been *jealous* of Martin? She wasn't an expert on casual sex by any means, but she was pretty sure that possessiveness and jealousy were not supposed to be part of the equation. Especially with a guy like Nathan, a man who lived in a single room at the back of someone else's property and who surfed and drank all day then hung out in bars chatting up women at night.

"I think you might be the most confusing man I've ever met."

He reached out and tucked a strand of hair behind her ear. "You're no walk in the park, either, your highness."

He leaned close and she didn't resist as he pulled her into his arms and kissed her, long and slow. He tasted of beer and salt and his skin felt very hot when she slid her arms around him. He spread his hands on her back and widened his stance and they stood there kissing like fervent teenagers, their hips and bellies and chests pressed together.

Finally he broke the kiss, sliding his hand down her arm to take her hand.

"Come shower with me," he said.

But she dug her heels in, resisting. He raised his eyebrows and she shook her head, feeling suddenly hugely out of her depth. She'd had a grand total of two lovers in her life, including him. She wasn't stupid, but she was very definitely inexperienced when it came to matters of sex and men and dating. She had no idea what was happening between them, what he wanted from her, what she could expect from him. Nothing? Hot sex for as long as it stayed fun? One more night? A week? A month?

"What is this?" she asked quietly. Probably that was breaking some mysterious rule of the dating world she didn't know about, but she had to know. She needed parameters, some kind of guidance, because she sensed that it would be very easy to let herself get swept away by Nathan's sexy body and boyish charm and incredible intensity.

"It is what it is, Lizzy. Fun in the sun, for as long as it lasts."

It was on the tip of her tongue to ask him about his jealousy, where that fit in to his easy-breezy view of things. But then he tugged on her hand again and she allowed him to lead her inside. She told herself it was because she was hot and a shower sounded wonderful and she wasn't ready to give up the sex yet.

It was almost the whole truth, too.

6

THEY WASHED EACH OTHER in the shower, then they crossed the yard to his studio and spent the afternoon naked in his bed.

Elizabeth had never felt so depraved, self-indulgent and decadent all at once. When she was with him, skin to skin, the outside world ceased to exist. There was only the suck and lick and pull of his mouth on her body, the glide of his fingers on her skin, the hard planes of his chest and back and belly, the fierce power of his thighs, the thick, satisfying length of him inside her.

After the sun had gone down they showered again. He pulled on a pair of jeans and laid a fire in the brick barbecue on the back lawn. She rummaged in the fridge and managed to cobble together a salad while he cooked steaks over the coals. They sat on a picnic blanket to eat, then stretched out in the twilight afterward, their plates pushed to one side, each of them nursing a cold bottle of beer.

They talked about books and movies and travel as the heat of the day slowly faded, and when she mentioned her teaching he peppered her with questions and seemed genuinely interested in her replies. She was surprised by how well-read he was, how well thought out his opinions were. It dawned on her that he was much more than a beautiful face and a hard body. She'd known he was smart—he was too quick on his feet to be anything but. She simply hadn't appreciated how sharp he was beneath the tan and the sand and the worn denim.

He asked why she'd chosen to teach in the public rather than the private system and listened as she told him about the special literacy course she'd run last year, and somehow the subject shifted to travel and she learned he'd surfed the coast of South America as well as Africa and spent nearly two months in Rome as a young man.

As the evening wore on she became more and more confused. On one hand, Nathan presented as a lazy layabout, a man who spent his days lolling in hammocks or riding waves. And yet he had clearly lived another life, a life outside of this small island and this very modest, slightly down-at-the-heel house.

Then there was the dark intensity he brought to the bedroom. This morning she'd scoffed at herself for reading things into the almost desperate way he held her and made love to her. Lying next to him under the stars, listening to him, she couldn't help wondering all over again. Because there was definitely more to this man than met the eye. Definitely.

She turned her head to look at him, besieged by questions—none of which she felt remotely entitled to ask. He hadn't asked her anything, after all. He hadn't even asked about Martin, and when she'd mentioned her parents' deaths during dinner he hadn't even offered the usual "sorry" before changing the subject. He hadn't volunteered anything about himself, either. In fact, she knew nothing about him except for his name and where he lived.

"You've got that look on your face again, Lizzy. I don't like it," Nathan said.

She'd thought he was stargazing, which was why she'd

been studying him so blatantly. But apparently he had twenty-twenty peripheral vision.

"What look is that?" she asked, matching his casual tone.

"That thinking look. I'm right, aren't I? You were thinking, weren't you?"

"It's rather difficult to stop, actually."

"Now that's where you're wrong. You just need something to distract you."

She watched as he put his beer down then rolled toward her and plucked her bottle from her hand.

"A distraction," she said. "Any suggestions?"

Warmth pooled low in her belly as Nathan's gaze slid over her body.

"Mmm. Let me see if I can think of anything," he murmured.

He leaned over her, one long leg sliding over hers as his hand found her breast and his mouth found her lips. They kissed deeply as his fingers teased at her nipple through the fabric of her dress, pinching, flicking, rubbing. She shifted restlessly, already anticipating the weight of his body on hers, the push of him inside her.

His hand left her breast and smoothed down her ribs, then her belly. He stopped when he reached her mound, simply resting his palm over it for long torturous seconds. She felt the heat from his hand flow into her body and she lifted her hips in silent invitation. He smiled against her mouth and began to pleat the fabric of her dress between his fingers, slowly gathering it up. When he had the bulk of it bunched around her hips he broke their kiss and began to lick and suck his way down her body, laving her neck, suckling her breasts, pushing her skirt higher still and dipping his tongue into the tiny well of her belly button.

She started to tremble with anticipation as his mouth moved

lower and lower. If he was going where she thought he was going, this was yet another area where she was woefully inexperienced. She'd thought about it—a lot—wondered what the heat of a mouth might feel like against the delicate, sensitive skin between her legs. But she'd never been bold enough to ask Martin to go down on her, and he'd never offered.

She gave a small gasp as Nathan's tongue slipped under the elastic on the waistband of her panties. He looked up at her, a smile on his face. She knew he could feel her trembling. He knew exactly how excited she was.

"You like this, Lizzy? If I'd known, I would have come visiting sooner."

"I don't know," she said before she could stop herself. "I've never done it before."

His hand tensed on her hip. "You're kidding."

She stared at him, determined not to say another betraying word. He already had too much power over her, she wasn't about to give him more.

He laid his cheek flat on her belly and hugged her hips to him. "Poor Lizzy. We'll have to make up for lost time, then."

He pressed a kiss to her mound through the silk of her underwear, then proceeded to torture her with his hands and fingers as he traced the edges of her panties, dropping kisses on her inner thighs, licking here, tasting there, but always avoiding the throbbing, hot place where she craved him the most.

She clenched and unclenched her hands, fighting the urge to simply lift her hips and thrust herself into his face. He was determined to tease her, and she was determined to withstand his teasing. If it killed her.

"How you doing up there?" he asked after a while, laughter in his voice.

"Just fine. You bastard," she panted.

He laughed outright and hooked a finger into her waistband. She lifted her hips as he pulled her panties off, the muscles of her belly and thighs tensing as he pushed her legs wide and settled between them. Here again he took his sweet time, looking his fill in the light of the almost-full moon. She desperately wanted to cover herself with her hand but she knew that would only amuse him even more.

"You're so pretty, Lizzy. I bet you taste good, too," he said.

She held on to the blanket for grim life as he lowered his face toward her. She felt his breath against her skin, then she gave a low, deep moan as his tongue lapped against her sex for the first time.

He laughed against her most tender flesh and licked her again.

It was incredible. Indescribable. Hot and wet and soft and hard all at once. He settled in, sucking, teasing, using his hands, driving her crazy with each stroke of his tongue.

She moaned and lifted her hips and drove her fingers into his hair and trembled with her approaching climax. Then he slid a finger inside her and she fell apart, pulsing and crying out and bucking her hips.

It seemed to last forever, and when it was over, he pressed a kiss to her thigh and undid his jeans and slid inside her while she was still trembling with aftershocks. Incredibly, she felt the excitement begin to build again as he stroked into her, his big body tense above her. As if her pleasure had fed his, he came quickly, his fingers digging into her hips as he shuddered out his release.

It was only after he'd withdrawn and she was lying boneless and spent on the blanket staring up at the stars that she thought about the fact that they were in his backyard, in the open, where anyone could see them if they cared to look over the fence or walk down the driveway.

"Bloody Nora," she said, flipping her skirt down and sitting up to look around in alarm.

Nathan took one look at her face and started laughing again.

"It's not funny. Anyone could have seen us. My God. What if the neighbors have children? We could have scarred them for life!"

"They're weekenders, Lizzy. They won't be down for another few weeks when school holidays start."

She shook her head at her own abandon. When she was with Nathan, every other consideration went out the window. It was more than a little scary.

He rolled close to her, nuzzling her neck.

"Anyway, I'd be more worried about them hearing us than seeing us. You make a lot of noise, Lizzy."

She gasped and hit his shoulder, trying to push him away.

"I do not!" she said, even though she was well aware she'd practically been howling at the moon not five minutes ago.

He didn't let her go. He kept pressing kisses against the soft skin beneath her ear, his tongue darting out occasionally to taste her.

"I like it. I like it a lot," he whispered against her skin.

And that quickly it was back, the irresistible, undeniable heat. She turned her mouth toward him, kissing him hungrily. Giving herself up yet again to the moment and letting everything else—her future, her father, her curiosity about Nathan—fall by the wayside.

NATE WOKE GASPING FOR air, his body drenched in sweat. The remnants of his dream still filled his head—the blood, Olivia pleading for him to help her, the dark pressing in on him, the sensation of being trapped. His heart was pounding against his breastbone and his thoughts kept slipping and sliding out of his control as his body tried to cope with an adrenaline-fueled flight-or-fight response that had nothing to do with the reality of the here and now.

Elizabeth stirred beside him. He rolled away from her. The last thing he wanted was to have to deal with her questions right now. She murmured in her sleep, then quieted.

He moved to the edge of the bed. At least he hadn't woken screaming. He should be grateful for small mercies. He'd be wired all day with the aftereffects of the adrenaline overload, of course. Edgy and tense. And tonight the odds were good that when he slipped into sleep the memories would be waiting for him again. Fear was great like that—the way it fed on itself until fear of fear itself became the biggest bogeyman of all.

He stood. He needed a shower.

He was halfway to the door when his phone started ringing. He fumbled beside the bed, finding his cell in the pocket of yesterday's jeans. Elizabeth's eyes flickered open as he checked the caller ID.

"Sam," he said into the phone.

Elizabeth tensed as she heard her father's name.

"Nate. I can't talk long. We're about to head out for off-coast drills. What's up?"

"I needed to talk to you," Nate said.

"Fire away."

Elizabeth sat up, pulling the sheet over her breasts. Her eyes were anxious as she watched him and Nate felt the enormous responsibility of what he was doing—brokering the first contact between father and long-lost child.

"Mate, there's someone here to see you. Her name is Elizabeth Mason—"

He broke off as Elizabeth touched his arm.

"My mother's name was Eleanor Whittaker. He won't recognize Mason."

"Her mother was Eleanor Whittaker," Nate said into the phone.

He paused, giving Sam the opportunity to jump in. He had no idea whether his friend even knew he had a child or if Elizabeth's facts were straight or—

"How did she find me?"

Sam didn't sound very surprised. Which probably meant he was well aware of Elizabeth's existence.

And yet he'd never contacted her. Nate frowned.

"I'm not sure. Maybe you should ask her yourself. She's here right now."

"No. Don't put her on." Sam's protest came so quickly it couldn't be anything but a knee-jerk response.

Aware of Elizabeth hanging on his every word, Nate stood and grabbed a towel off the end of the bed, wedging the phone between shoulder and ear while he wrapped the towel around his hips. He made brief eye contact with Elizabeth as he headed for the door.

"Give me a minute," he said, then he strode outside.

He waited until he was in the far corner of the yard and out of earshot before speaking again.

"What's going on, Sam?"

"Listen, I can't do this right now. The race kicks off in a couple of weeks. I need to have my head in the game." Sam sounded panicky.

"She's flown halfway around the world to find you."

"I didn't ask her to come."

"Sam, she's your *daughter*."

He'd known Sam for nearly ten years, ever since they'd crewed together on a mutual friend's boat. They'd sailed together, gotten drunk together, and for the past four months they'd been living together. If anyone had asked, Nate would have said Sam was an honorable guy—completely obsessed with the sea, sure, but a decent guy. Nate couldn't believe that the man he knew was prepared to simply blow his daughter off without even talking to her.

"I don't need the distraction right now, Nate. This is a big one. We've got a real chance of winning this year, which means we'll contest the Transpac and maybe even the Fastnet."

"Jesus, Sam, can you hear yourself? You're talking about a bunch of races and I'm telling you your daughter is here, wanting to meet you for the first time in her freaking life."

There was a short silence on the other end of the phone. Then Sam swore.

"All right. Put her on. I'll talk to her."

"Bloody generous of you."

"Give me a break, will you? You caught me on the hop."

"Right."

Nate stared at the open door to the studio. He was of two minds about handing the phone over. He'd seen the hope in Elizabeth's eyes when she heard who was calling. There was no way she wasn't going to be disappointed by her father's lackluster response. Hell, Nate was disappointed, and he had no vested interest in their relationship whatsoever. Sam had always been a difficult bugger, a loner with precious few social skills. But Elizabeth was his daughter.

Nate shrugged impatiently. None of this was any of his business—there was no reason whatsoever for him to feel protective and indignant on Elizabeth's behalf. Just because he'd slept with her a few times didn't make her his responsibility. He could barely get through the night without waking in a sweat and shaking like a baby. He had enough on his own plate without taking on someone else's problems.

He lifted the phone to his ear again.

"Give me a second. I'll go find her."

"How come she's hanging around at your place at eight in the morning, anyway?" Sam asked suspiciously.

Nate didn't bother answering. A man who could barely

muster the interest to talk to his own daughter had no right to ask those kinds of questions.

Elizabeth was pulling on her clothes when he entered. He offered her the phone.

"He wants to talk to you," he said.

She hesitated a moment, her gaze searching his face. Then she took a deep breath, squared her shoulders and reached for the phone.

"Elizabeth speaking."

Good manners dictated that Nate make himself scarce, but he wanted to make sure Sam was behaving himself first. He watched her face carefully as she listened to Sam on the other end of the phone.

"Nathan told me you were crewing for the big race. I'm more than happy to fly up to Sydney—"

She frowned as Sam said something on the other end to cut her off. Nate could guess what it was. Elizabeth lifted a hand and rubbed her forehead with her fingertips.

"I see."

There was a world of disappointment in those two words. Nate watched the expectation and anticipation slowly drain out of her. They hadn't spoken about it—he deliberately hadn't asked, and she hadn't offered—but he knew she'd had high hopes of her long-lost father. What person wouldn't? She'd probably imagined getting to know him, perhaps finding out they had things in common, slowly forging a bond....

"Of course. I understand," she said.

Nate headed for the door. He didn't want to play witness to her disappointment. He didn't want to feel for her. He didn't want to feel anything—had spent the past few months working damned hard, in fact, to achieve a state of numb indifference.

He went into the house and made coffee, telling himself

all the while that Elizabeth was an adult. She could look after herself.

He was dressed and pouring milk into his coffee when the bead curtain on the rear door rattled. He turned to find Elizabeth standing there. She'd pulled her hair into a ponytail low on the back of her head and her face looked very pale.

"Thanks for that. I appreciate it." She handed over his phone.

"You want some coffee?" he asked. Because no way was he asking if she was okay, or what Sam had said. He wasn't getting involved. He refused to.

"No. I'm fine. I might head back to the hotel, actually. Thanks for dinner and…everything."

She turned toward the door.

"You know your way back okay?" he asked, even though he knew she did, since she'd found him yesterday.

"Yes, thank you."

She offered him a small, polite smile before exiting. Nate listened to the beads rattle against one another. Then he took his coffee to the kitchen table and sat.

She was upset. God only knew what Sam had said to her. Some bullshit about how important the race was, or some other piss-poor justification for his lack of interest.

He pulled the morning paper toward himself and flicked to the cartoon page. He read all his favorites, then folded the page in half to tackle the crossword puzzle.

And through it all, he couldn't get Elizabeth out of his mind.

She deserved better. She'd come here looking for her father, for Pete's sake.

Before he could think twice, Nate pushed away from the kitchen table. There was no sign of her in the street. He lengthened his stride as he reached the track to the beach. He spotted her straightaway once he hit the sand, a lone figure trudging toward town with her sandals in her hand.

"Elizabeth," he called.

She paused and looked over her shoulder. He slowed to an easy lope as he crossed the final distance between them.

"You got plans for the day?" he asked when he reached her side.

She frowned as though she didn't understand what he was asking. "Plans?"

"Are you doing anything?"

"Oh." She blinked. "I was thinking of finding an Internet café so I could check my e-mail. But other than that…"

She shrugged. He hated the closed-down look behind her eyes. Bloody Sam. When Nate saw him next he was going to kick his ass.

"There's a good northeasterly coming through. Great day to take the cat out, if you're game."

"You have a cat?"

"A catamaran, the *Rubber Ducky*. A Hobie 16. You ever sailed before, Lizzy?"

"No."

He slung his arm around her shoulders. "Another first, then. What do you say?"

She looked confused for a moment, then she made an embarrassed sound and tried to wriggle out from under his arm.

"Trust you to bring that up. I knew I shouldn't have said anything."

"Your secrets are safe with me, Lizzy. I promise."

She stopped struggling. He tugged on her ponytail.

"Come on, it'll be fun."

"There's that word again," she said, her face downturned as she stared at something on the ground.

He tugged on her hair again. "Don't knock it till you've tried it. Are you in or what, Lizzy?"

She thought about it for a moment. Then she lifted her face and met his eyes.

"Yes, I'm in."

"Duck!" Nate yelled.

Elizabeth clapped a hand onto the ridiculous floppy sun hat he'd insisted she wear and flattened herself against the trampoline as the boom swung over her head. Her safety vest shifted awkwardly, pressing underneath her armpits. She tugged it down again when she heard the hiss of ropes sliding through pulleys as Nate worked to tie the boom in its new position.

"You can come up now, Lizzy."

She knew without looking that he was laughing at her. He'd been laughing at her all morning. As a sailor, she apparently made a fantastic clown. The stupid hat and cumbersome life vest and pale pink zinc cream he'd spread over her nose didn't help much in that area, she suspected.

She couldn't help smiling in response, however. It was hard not to when they were racing across the water, Nate's elegant catamaran skating across the surface of the waves, its twin hulls slapping salt spray into the air. The deep aquamarine of the ocean beneath them, the almost-painful cornflower-blue of the sky overhead, the warmth of the sun, Nate's laughter—it was exhilarating, there was no other word for it.

The perfect antidote to the phone call from her father.

Instead of sitting upright again, Elizabeth rolled onto her side and edged toward the front of the boat. The black trampoline fabric was hot beneath her legs as she lay full length and peered over the front beam, staring down at the sea as it whipped past.

To say that her father had been unenthusiastic about her appearance in his life was putting it mildly. He'd actually sounded put out when he spoke to her, as though he'd been burdened with an unwanted responsibility at the worst possible time. She was an inconvenience, apparently. Not that he'd said as much. But she could read between the lines. She'd offered to fly to Sydney to meet him, but he'd claimed he was too busy drilling before the big race. She'd agreed to wait until he could fly back to Melbourne after the race finished, but she was in two minds now about whether she would wait for him or not.

He'd known about her. All along, he'd known he had a daughter, and yet he'd never tried to contact her. It was a body blow, there was no denying it. She'd fooled herself that she'd come without expectations, because the reality was that she'd hoped that there'd been some reason for his absence in her life. Some proof that her grandfather's judgment that her father was "not someone they wanted involved in her life" was wrong. But apparently her father wasn't even vaguely curious about his child born on the other side of the world.

She stretched her arm out and trailed it in the icy water, feeling the tug against her fingers as it resisted her invasion.

Maybe this whole trip had been a huge mistake. A gross miscalculation on her behalf. Maybe she should cut her losses and go home now, save herself from further rejection.

"Come back up this end, Lizzy. We're going to tack and head downwind and I need your weight back here."

"How flattering," she said.

She pushed herself up onto her hands and knees and made her way to the rear of the trampoline where Nathan sat at the helm, one hand on the tiller, the other on the line that controlled the boom.

She felt uniquely inelegant as she plopped down beside him in her borrowed board shorts and T-shirt. Fabric was bunched around her middle where she'd cinched his too-large shorts tight and the fluorescent orange safety vest made her feel ten times her normal size.

Nate reached across to tug her hat lower on her face.

"Careful with that complexion, Lizzy. And when we run downwind, we have to keep the bow up out of the water to avoid pitchpoling. That's why I need you back here with me."

"What's pitchpoling?"

"It's when the bow pushes down under the force of the wind so much that it dips under the water."

He made a tipping motion with his hand to illustrate.

"Are you saying that the whole boat could flip over?" she asked, alarmed.

"Relax. I haven't pitchpoled the *Rubber Ducky* for years."

"Dear God," she said under her breath, glancing around the small, sleek catamaran with new eyes. It had all seemed so innocuous up until now.

"Here," Nathan said, and she found herself holding the tiller as he scrambled forward to do something with the sail.

"Isn't this a little like asking a passenger to volunteer to fly the plane?" she asked nervously. The tiller vibrated beneath her hand with the force of their movement through the water.

"How are you going to learn to sail if you don't get some time at the helm?" Nate asked, his deft fingers threading rope through a cleat.

"Learn to sail?" she squeaked. "Are you kidding?"

She stared up at the mast towering overhead with its acres and acres of taut sail. Never in a million years would she feel confident enough to captain such a delicately balanced piece of engineering.

"What did you think this was? A leisure cruise?"

He sat beside her. "Okay, so we're heading downwind at the moment…"

He explained the theory of tacking to her, pointing out the tightly bound boom—close hauled, in sailor speak—and showing her how they were keeping the wind on one side of the *Ducky* or the other as they worked their way across the bay. Then he took her through a tack, talking her through each stage and forcibly pushing her head down when she became so absorbed she forgot to duck as the boom swept from one side of the boat to the other.

"I did it!" she whooped as the sail bellied out over her head and the *Ducky* started to move again.

"Yes, Captain, you did," Nate said, offering her a salute.

After a couple more tacks they sailed back to shore. Elizabeth watched, fascinated, as Nate lifted the rudders and glided the boat straight up onto the sand.

"And that doesn't hurt the thingies at all?" she asked.

"The hulls? Nope. They're made out of superstrong fiberglass. Of course, we probably don't want to beach on a chunk of rock."

She accepted his help to scramble off the trampoline and stood upright for the first time in hours, a big, goofy smile on her face, her board shorts dripping with seawater.

"That was wonderful. I can't understand why I've never done it before," she said.

"Maybe because you live on a little island where it rains most of the year?"

She wrinkled her zinc-covered nose at him. Nate stepped closer and for a moment she thought he was going to kiss her, but he reached for the clasp on her life vest and worked it loose.

"Oh. Thanks."

The vest loosened around her waist and she shrugged out of it.

"Thank heaven. It's like wearing a straitjacket," she said as she threw it on the trampoline.

Nate shrugged out of his own vest. She couldn't help admiring the way his wet T-shirt clung to his chest.

"Now, the not-so-fun part—packing up," he said.

She worked alongside him to bring the sail down, then carried it with him up to the clubhouse where they washed it down with freshwater to remove any salt spray. Once it was dry, they rolled it and stowed it in a long canvas bag. Then she helped him coil ropes, copying his expert moves in her own fumbling way.

"Sailing can be addictive, so you'd better be careful," Nate said as he tied off a coil of rope and dropped it onto the trampoline. "Sam's like that—not happy unless he's on the water."

It was the first time he'd ever mentioned her father and she shot him a look. His face was absolutely neutral as he checked to make sure the rudders were locked upright. As though they were discussing the weather or something equally banal.

"Sam'll do pretty much anything to get out there," he said. "A lot of small yacht deliveries for rich guys who need their boats sailed from one port to another, crewing with bigger yachts when the work comes up. He's more than happy to spend days out on the water on his own. Which probably explains why he's a taciturn bastard at the best of times."

It took her a moment to understand what he was doing: letting her know that her father's rejection wasn't personal, that he was an isolate by nature. She stroked her finger along the silky weave of the rope she was coiling, assessing the conversation she'd had with her father from this new perspective.

If her father was a shy man, a loner, socially awkward…it was possible that his first response to contact from a long-lost child might be retreat.

"Thanks," she said quietly.

Nate wiped his brow with the hem of his T-shirt, leaving a pink smear on the fabric from the zinc across his nose and cheeks. "Better go see if there's anyone in the clubhouse who can give us a lift back up to the racks. Unless you're hiding muscles I don't know about, Lizzy?"

"No, I'm afraid not."

"Didn't think so."

She watched as he made his way up the sand. He'd gone out of his way to be kind to her today, taking her out on the water to distract her from her disillusionment then offering her some insight into her father's character so she could better understand his behavior. Nathan was clearly uncomfortable with having that kindness acknowledged, however. She remembered how he'd told her he didn't want to get involved in any *This Is Your Life* situations that first time they'd met—then proceeded to follow her to her car and reassure her, as well as make contact with her father on her behalf.

She realized she was staring after him like a love-struck teenager and forced herself to turn away and concentrate on coiling the last rope. She needed to tread carefully. She'd already acknowledged that he was different from any other man she'd ever met. He'd introduced her to a world of sensual pleasure she'd only ever suspected existed, and he'd been very kind to her, in his own quiet, low-key way. Then there was the intense, intelligent, intriguing conversation they'd shared last night....

She was smart enough to know that all those things together were a pretty deadly combination, no matter how many times she assured herself she understood that he was a good-time guy and this was only a holiday fling.

The sound of masculine laughter heralded Nathan's return with three other men, all of whom were tanned and fit-looking, dressed casually in T-shirts and board shorts like Nathan.

"Lizzy, this is David, Gary and Steve," Nathan said.

"Hi," Elizabeth said, offering them all a wave of her hand.

She tugged on the hem of her soggy, oversize T-shirt, aware she probably looked like something the cat had dragged in.

As though he sensed her self-consciousness, Nate draped an arm around her shoulders and dropped a kiss onto her nose before ushering her to one side.

"Stand back and let us men do our thing," he said in a deliberately deep, gravelly voice.

"Should I cheer you on? Or maybe squeal a little?" she offered drily.

Nate stripped off his wet T-shirt, tossing it over to her.

"Save the squealing for later," he said with a wink.

The other men laughed, and Elizabeth rolled her eyes as they each grabbed a corner of the boat and hefted. Muscles rippled down Nate's arms and back, and she forgot what she'd been about to say in response.

She followed them as they carried the catamaran up the beach. She couldn't take her eyes off Nate. And it wasn't just because of his body.

Be very careful, Elizabeth.

But it was hard to listen to common sense when the sun was shining and she was walking on the wild side for the first time in her life.

7

NATE WOKE TO FIND Elizabeth curled into his side again. Even as his cock rejoiced, his shoulders tensed.

He shouldn't have invited her to stay for dinner last night. The sailing lesson was one thing, but he shouldn't have cooked her dinner, then pulled her into the studio afterward and peeled off her clothes and laid his body over hers. Definitely he shouldn't have wrapped his arms around her afterward and fallen asleep nuzzling her neck.

What he should have done was send her home and nipped this thing in the bud. She was a good person—a nice person. He didn't want to hurt her. But it was inevitable if they kept seeing each other like this.

The problem was, he really liked her. The sex was fantastic, and she was smart and funny and she didn't play games.

And he was a guy who could barely get through the night without nightmares. A guy who'd retreated to the far corner of his own life in an attempt to stop himself from going completely nuts—if it hadn't happened already.

He had no business starting something with her that he couldn't finish. He had nothing to offer beyond sex, and somehow, despite his best intentions, this thing between them was already moving past that.

So. It was time to pull the pin. She might hate him for it in the short term, but she'd thank him in the long run.

Having made his decision, he told himself to get out of bed and start putting distance between them. Instead, he smoothed his hand down her shoulder, savoring the cool silk of her hair against his fingers. Then he lowered his head and inhaled the warm smell of her skin—sweet, with just a hint of her citrusy perfume lingering.

There was no getting around it. He'd found more peace, more comfort in her arms the past few nights than he had for months. Ridiculous as it seemed after such a short time, he was going to miss her.

Get out of bed. Get out of bed. Get out of bed.

He knew the voice in his head was smart and rational, but he didn't move. Instead, he waited another half hour until she woke, her eyes fluttering, a slight frown on her face. She smiled when she saw he was awake already, the warmth in her eyes making him hard and uneasy at the same time.

"Hello," she said.

"Hi."

She glanced down and noticed his hard-on.

"And good morning to you, too," she said.

She smoothed a hand down his belly. He caught it just before she wrapped her fingers around his cock and forced himself to say what needed to be said.

"Listen. I have to leave the island for a few days," he said.

She stilled and he knew that she understood the unspoken message behind his casual words.

She withdrew her hand. "Are you, um, heading off today?" she asked, her tone carefully light.

"This afternoon, most likely," he lied.

She nodded. "Well. Have a good trip."

"Yeah. Thanks. I will."

It was a ludicrously stiff and formal conversation to be having while naked, lying side by side in bed. He threw off the sheet and stood. Elizabeth's dress and underwear were folded neatly on the chair in the corner and he passed them to her. She gave him a small smile of thanks that didn't reach her eyes.

He turned away and pulled on a pair of cargo shorts.

"Might go make some coffee," he said.

He left her to get dressed, crossing the dewy grass to the house, cursing himself every step of the way for being about as subtle as a sledgehammer.

But he only had to remember the flash of hurt he'd seen in her eyes to know he'd done the right thing.

He was pushing open the back door when someone spoke behind him.

"Nate."

He looked over his shoulder. Jarvie stood near the corner of the house, a wary expression on his face. His business partner looked tired, older than when Nate had last seen him. It took Nate a moment to find his voice.

"What are you doing here?"

Jarvie lifted his hand and Nate saw he was holding another one of those damned envelopes.

"I brought your mail."

Nate stepped back onto the lawn. "Last time I looked, there were a bunch of people they paid to do that."

"Last time I looked, people actually opened their mail."

"You've got my vote. Do what you like with the business."

"It's your company, too, Nate. I can't make all the decisions on my own."

Jesus. They'd been over all this a million times. He stared at the ground, his jaw tight, not saying anything. He didn't want to think about any of this. Couldn't. All of it—the company,

BUSINESS REPLY MAIL
FIRST-CLASS MAIL   PERMIT NO. 717   BUFFALO, NY

POSTAGE WILL BE PAID BY ADDRESSEE

THE READER SERVICE
PO BOX 1867
BUFFALO NY 14240-9952

NO POSTAGE
NECESSARY
IF MAILED
IN THE
UNITED STATES

Send For
2 FREE BOOKS
Today!

I accept your offer!

Please send me two
free Harlequin® Blaze®
novels and two mystery
gifts (gifts worth about $10).
I understand that these books
are completely free—even
the shipping and handling will
be paid—and I am under no
obligation to purchase anything, ever,
as explained on the back of this card.

About how many NEW paperback fiction books have you purchased in the past 3 months?

❑ 0-2   ❑ 3-6   ❑ 7 or more
E7UH   **E7UT**   **E7U5**

151/351 HDL

Please Print

FIRST NAME

LAST NAME

ADDRESS

APT.#   CITY

Visit us online at
www.ReaderService.com

STATE/PROV.   ZIP/POSTAL CODE

H-B-07/10   Detach card and mail today! No stamp needed. ▲ © 2010 HARLEQUIN ENTERPRISES LIMITED. ® and ™ are trademarks owned and used by the trademark owner and/or its licensee. Printed in the U.S.A.

his old life—belonged to a man who didn't exist anymore. And Jarvie knew that. Yet he kept sending mail and now he was here, asking for something Nate didn't have it in his power to give.

"We can't keep going on like this. The company works best when we're both there. We need you," Jarvie said.

"Believe me, you don't. I gave you power of attorney over my share of the business. Just do whatever you need to do."

"It's not that simple and you know it. You're the one who wrote the software. No one knows it better than you. We've had requests for new features, modifications…"

"Hire more programmers."

"They're not you. They don't know Smartsell like you do."

"They'll work it out. It's not rocket science."

Nate could feel himself getting angrier and angrier. Why couldn't Jarvie leave him the hell alone? He knew why Nate was here. He knew everything. So why did he keep pushing and pushing?

"Nate—"

"You think I want this? You think I like living like this? Do you have any idea—" He broke off, breathing hard. He clenched and unclenched his hands, hot pressure building at the back of his eyes.

"Listen, I know it's tough, man. But you can't just lock yourself away down here. You need to come back up to the city, start seeing that doctor again. She was helping, right? And maybe if you came into work a few days a week, things would start looking up again."

Looking up again.

Right.

Nate laughed. Jarvie had no idea. Standing there talking about Nate returning to the city and returning to work. As though there was nothing in the world stopping Nate from doing any of those things if he wanted to.

But, of course, as far as Jarvie was concerned, there wasn't. He didn't understand that after six months Nate still had to anesthetize himself with beer or vodka to get to sleep each night. Jarvie had no idea that all it took was the screech of tires or the wrong combination of noises or simply Nate letting his guard down and he was in the middle of a flashback to those long hours in the car, at the mercy of his own messed-up subconscious. Jarvie didn't have his little sister's voice in his head, pleading with him to do something, anything, to stop the pain.

He didn't have to live with the knowledge that he'd taken the life of the one person he loved more than any other in all the world.

Nate stared at his old friend, his body shaking with the force of his fury. For a moment he teetered on the brink of giving in to the urge to pound on something, anything, to release the anger and self-hate and fear inside himself. Then he reminded himself that this was Jarvie, his oldest friend, his business partner, and even if Jarvie didn't understand, he was here for the right reasons.

"You should get out of here," Nate said, turning away.

Jarvie stepped into his path. "You have to stop running from this, man."

"Get out of the way."

"Not until you listen to me."

"Move," Nate said between his teeth.

"No."

Nate's hand curled into a fist, his arm muscles bunching, his shoulders squaring. If Jarvie wanted a fight, he'd come to the right place.

"Nathan, don't!" Suddenly Elizabeth was between them,

her hand on his arm. She was barefoot, her hair a tangle around her head.

He had no idea how long she'd been watching, how much she'd heard. Jarvie released his grip and Nate took a step away from his old friend.

"Don't come again," Nate said.

Then he turned and fled the accusation in his old friend's eyes.

ELIZABETH WATCHED NATE walk around the corner of the house. She couldn't believe he'd been on the verge of a fight before she'd intervened.

"Shit," Nate's visitor said, the single word full of frustration and regret.

She glanced at him. He was about the same age as Nate, dressed casually but expensively in designer jeans and a Paul Smith shirt with striped cuffs.

He returned her regard, his gray gaze flicking up and down her body assessingly.

Since she didn't know what else to do she offered her hand.

"I'm Elizabeth Mason," she said.

When in doubt, be polite.

He stared at her hand as though he didn't quite know what to do with it before reaching out to shake it.

"Jarvie Roberts."

"I'm sure Nate will be back shortly," she said.

Because surely he would be. He couldn't leave his friend hanging like this.

Jarvie smiled cynically. "No, he won't. He won't come back until he knows I've cleared out."

"Oh."

Jarvie's gaze slid over her again, then he bent and collected the envelope from the ground. He handed it to her.

"Would you mind giving this to him?"

"Certainly."

"Thanks, I appreciate it," he said. He raised his hand in farewell as he strode up the driveway.

Elizabeth sighed and pushed her hair away from her forehead.

What in hell had all that been about?

She looked at the envelope in her hands. She hadn't heard much of the heated conversation, but she'd heard enough to gather that Nate was partners in some sort of business with the other man and that he'd recently walked away from it. She eyed the logo on the envelope. Smartsell. She'd never heard of it, but that didn't mean anything.

Nathan didn't strike her as a man who'd abandon a business on a whim. Even though her first impression had been that he was a lazy, feckless beach bum, she knew him a little better now.

She went into the kitchen and propped the envelope against the salt and pepper shakers on the kitchen table so he would see it as soon as he came in. As she was turning away, her gaze fell on a magazine rack in the far corner, overflowing with similar-looking envelopes. She stepped closer to examine them. Sure enough, they all bore the Smartsell logo.

Confused and worried, she walked to the beach in search of Nate.

She told herself she was being stupid, that Nate did not want her chasing him. He'd cut her loose this morning, in no uncertain terms. She might not be very experienced with men, but she recognized a kiss-off when she heard one.

Still, she walked to the waterline and shaded her eyes, looking up and down the beach for him.

His whole body had been trembling when she touched his arm to stop the fight. And the look in his eyes...

Her gut told her that something was very wrong, and she

was worried about him. Maybe that made her foolish, but so be it. She could be embarrassed about it later, when she'd assured herself he was all right.

She walked along the beach for fifteen minutes in both directions, then she went to the pub and checked both the beer garden and the public bar. There was no sign of Nate anywhere, and the barman, Trevor, said he hadn't seen him.

Which left her at a standstill. She didn't know Nate well enough to guess where else he might go. Which pretty much said everything, really.

Just leave it, Elizabeth. He's not your responsibility. You had some good sex, he cut you loose, that's it. Let it go.

Good advice, but it didn't stop her from descending the stairs to the main bar earlier than usual that night, hoping Nathan would be there. He wasn't and she was on edge all evening, waiting for him to appear. By eleven he hadn't and she figured he wasn't going to. She went upstairs to her room and told herself it was just as well.

Her island fling was well and truly over.

NATE SUCKED DOWN THE LAST of his beer and threw the empty bottle onto the grass beneath the hammock. It clinked against another empty bottle, which wasn't exactly a miracle since he'd been drinking heavily since he returned to the house in the late afternoon and the lawn was littered with bottles.

Despite all the beer, the agitated, unsettled feeling still gripped his chest and gut, as it had all day.

Bloody Jarvie. Coming down here, ruining Nate's peace. He'd given the guy carte blanche to do whatever he wanted with the business—why couldn't he just piss off and leave Nate to what was left of his life? Why did he have to keep inserting himself into things, reminding Nate of the way things used to be?

It had taken Nate months to develop a routine that got him

through the days and the nights. After too many hangovers
to count he'd finally discovered the perfect amount of beer
to consume to achieve an undisturbed night's sleep without
making the next day a disaster. Between the beer and the
surfing and the occasional hook-up with a warm and willing
woman from town, he'd survived the past four months. Just.

Then Jarvie had barged in this morning with his demands,
bringing Nate's old life with him.

He closed his eyes and pressed his fingers against his eyelids, thinking about the envelope Jarvie had left on his kitchen
table and all that it represented.

*Why can't he understand? I don't want it. I don't want any
of it anymore.*

The success he'd worked so hard to achieve. The big house
and expensive car and invitations from people who knew
people. None of it meant anything anymore.

It wasn't like he hadn't tried to pick up the pieces after the
accident. He'd gone back to work. He'd even tried to drive
once his concussion specialist had told him he was clear to
do so.

Nausea burned the back of Nate's throat and he swallowed
urgently. It was pathetic, but the memory of the afternoon
he'd tried to get behind the wheel again still had the power to
freak him out. Opening the car door. The smell of leather and
expensive electronics. The steering wheel, the gearshift, the
windshield. He'd slid into the driver's seat and been instantly
transported to that night. The sound of screeching rubber, the
smash of rending metal and shattering glass, the explosion of
the airbags. The blood. The pain. The helplessness.

Nate gripped the edge of the hammock and swung his legs
to the ground. He braced his legs wide and stared hard at the
grass, his body tense, his breath coming fast as he battled with
remembered panic and fear.

He closed his eyes, but nothing could block out the sound

of Olivia's screaming. She was always there, in the back of his mind. Dying over and over again. And there was nothing he could do to help her or stop the pain or soothe her.

Anger and despair welled up inside him. This was Jarvie's fault. If he hadn't come... Why couldn't he leave Nate alone?

It took five minutes to get the nausea under control. Nate pushed himself to his feet and crossed to the house, heading straight for the fridge. He needed more beer to drown Olivia out. He needed to drink until he was numb again.

He stared at the empty shelves in the fridge. It took him a few seconds to understand there was nothing left to drink. He swore under his breath and pulled the freezer door open, looking for the bottle of vodka he kept there. He dragged it out and swore again when he saw there was barely an inch left.

How had he let that happen? He always had beer and vodka on hand. Always. He slammed the freezer door shut and leaned his forehead against the cool white metal. He hadn't restocked because he'd been so busy thinking about Elizabeth, fantasizing about getting her naked again, that it hadn't seemed important.

Stupid. So stupid.

He'd have to go into town, buy some more beer. Enough to get him through the night. He headed for the door but the clock on the kitchen wall caught his eye. It was past twelve. Which meant the pub would be closed for the night.

He stood frozen in the middle of the kitchen, panic fluttering in his chest. He needed that beer. How was he going to get through the night without it?

He walked into the living room and sank onto the couch. Maybe if he tried to sleep now, before the beer buzz wore off, he'd be able to get past this shit that Jarvie had stirred up. Then tomorrow it would be business as usual, back to his routine.

He'd stock up on alcohol again, make sure he had backup this time. Batten down the hatches and wait for things to settle.

He lay down and rolled to face the back of the couch. His legs were too long and he bent his knees and drew them up. He had a sudden flash of how he must look—a grown man, huddled on the couch like a child.

Pathetic. So freaking weak.

He wrapped his arms around himself as the trembling began. He could hear Olivia screaming. He squeezed his eyes tightly closed and prayed to whoever might be listening to let him make it to dawn.

ELIZABETH WOKE FROM A DEEP sleep to the sound of someone pounding on her hotel-room door. She sat up with a start and reached for the robe she'd left lying across the end of her bed. The glowing bedside clock told her it was three o'clock as she crossed to the door.

She was pretty sure she knew who it was, but she stood on tiptoes and looked through the spy hole just in case. Nate stood on the other side, his face downturned as he leaned one arm against the door, his expression distorted by the fish-eye lens.

She twisted the lock and opened the door. Nate dropped his arm and straightened.

"Hey."

"What's going on?" she asked.

She could smell beer. He was glassy-eyed, with a fine sheen of sweat on his face. He smiled, but it didn't even come close to reaching his eyes.

"Can I come in?" he asked.

She stepped to one side silently, watching him carefully as he entered her room. Something was going on. He'd clearly been drinking—hardly new—but there was something else. Something wrong behind his eyes.

"How about I make us a coffee?" she said.

She turned toward the small counter in the corner but Nate came up behind her and slid his arm around her, his hand sliding unerringly onto her breast. He began massaging her through the silk of her robe, his hips pressing against her backside as he nuzzled the nape of her neck.

Impossible to stop herself from responding to his touch, but there was something so desperate about the way he held her, as though he was trying to merge his body with hers. He started to peel off her robe, his movements jerky and impatient.

"Nate. Has something happened?" she asked.

She twisted in his arms so that she could see his face but he immediately ducked his head and started kissing her, forcing her head back on her neck with his need.

His hands cupped her backside through her robe, lifting her against his hips as he rubbed himself against her over and over. His whole body was trembling, his muscles bunched as he held her tight.

Emotion closed her throat. He hadn't said a word, but she could feel the pain in him—he *vibrated* with it like a struck tuning fork. She wrapped her arms around him and smoothed her palms up and down his back, trying to reassure and calm him.

"It's okay, Nate," she murmured against his mouth. "Whatever it is, it's okay."

His breath seemed to get stuck in his throat then and he broke their kiss, pressing his face into the soft skin beneath her ear, his arms as hard as steel as he held her close. The trembling increased and he made a strangled noise in the back of his throat. She had no idea what to say or do, so she followed her instincts, soothing him with her hands, offering him what reassurance she could.

"It's okay, Nate," she said again. "You're safe here."

She rested one hand on top of his bowed head, the other

in the middle of his back, holding him to her as tightly as he was holding her. She wasn't going anywhere and she wanted him to know it.

Slowly the trembling faded. She felt Nate come back into himself and a new kind of tension took over his body. He started to push her away, no doubt feeling self-conscious now that the moment of crisis had passed. She didn't give him a chance to withdraw; instead, she encouraged him toward the bed.

"Sit down," she instructed.

He hesitated a moment. She knew he was trying to formulate an excuse so he could leave. She pushed him toward the bed.

"Go on," she said.

His face was shuttered when he looked at her. Then he took a step backward and sat on the bed. She knelt and pulled off his boots and socks, then she tugged at the waistband on his jeans and unzipped his fly. He leaned back as she peeled his jeans over his hips.

"Lie down," she said.

This time he obeyed as meekly as a child, shuffling over to make room for her. She lay down beside him and drew his head onto her chest, wrapping her arms around as much of him as she could hold. He lay there tensely for a beat, resisting the comfort she offered. Then his body relaxed and he turned his face into her breast, his breath coming in noisy gusts.

She felt dampness against her skin and knew he was crying. Tears stung her own eyes but she blinked them away and simply held him, her hands smoothing soothing circles on his back.

After a while Nate's grip softened. His breathing became deep and slow. She brushed the hair from his forehead and looked down into his face, still tight with anguish even though he was asleep.

Whatever was wrong, she was deeply touched that he'd come to her, even if he'd had to dress it up as sexual need to allow himself to do so. Which was crazy when she considered how long they'd known each other.

A warning bell sounded in her mind. She silenced it. Right now, Nate needed her. That was the only important consideration. Reality could wait until morning.

8

NATE WOKE TO DARKNESS and the soft rise and fall of Elizabeth's breast beneath his cheek. It took a moment for memory to fully return. Scorching heat rose up his chest and into his face as he remembered the way he'd pounded on her door and then jumped on her like a desperate madman. God only knew what she must think of him. It was a wonder she hadn't called security and had him thrown out.

He eased away from her until he was on his back, his head on a pillow instead of the cushioning warmth of her body. His face felt stiff from his tears. He ground his teeth together, furious and humiliated in equal measure.

He'd lost it last night. Big-time. Not since the early days after the accident had he been such a basket case.

He almost laughed as a thought occurred to him: if Jarvie could have seen him last night, there was no way he'd want him back in the business. Maybe next time the night terrors struck he should record it and send the disk to Jarvie for his edification. No doubt he'd never be bothered again once his old friend understood exactly how screwed up Nate really was.

"How are you feeling?"

The gentle inquiry came out of the darkness. He tensed.

He'd planned on being long gone by the time she woke. Save them both from the awkwardness of having to look each other in the eye after his meltdown.

"Do you want some water? Maybe some aspirin?"

"I'm fine. Thanks."

There was a short silence. Then he heard her inhale.

"Want to talk about it?"

He smiled grimly. Did he want to talk about it—the million dollar question. Everybody who claimed any friendship with him had been eager to talk in those early days. They'd all wanted to "be there" for him. And all he'd wanted to do was forget.

But he couldn't simply pull on his jeans and bugger off, not when he'd cried like a baby in Elizabeth's arms. He owed her something. Some explanation, at least.

"Sorry for barging in on you like that. It won't happen again," he said.

"I didn't ask for an apology, Nathan. But if you don't want to talk, I understand."

Her hand found his arm, then his hand. She slid her palm against his and wove their fingers together. She didn't say anything further, simply squeezed his hand comfortingly.

Hot emotion choked his throat for the second time. He swallowed, the sound audible in the quiet room.

Bloody hell. He really was losing it. Might as well hand his cojones over now.

"I noticed that some of the other catamarans had two sails up yesterday. Is that normal or are they different from the *Rubber Ducky?*" Elizabeth asked.

For a moment he was thrown by the abrupt change of subject. Then he understood what she was doing: giving him some breathing room. He squeezed her hand and she returned the gentle pressure.

"You're talking about a jib," he said. His voice caught and

he cleared his throat. "They make the cat more maneuverable and help with tacking. We had a good northerly the other day, though, so I didn't bother rigging it."

"Right. So when you're sailing alone, how do you manage it as well as the main sail?"

"You cleat the main sail first, then move forward to set the jib…"

They talked sailing for a few minutes. The faintest tinge of light was starting to creep beneath the blind. Gradually the tension in his chest eased. He turned his head and studied Elizabeth's profile, barely discernible in the dim light. Her small nose, the shape of her mouth and slope of her cheek.

He made a decision and returned his gaze to the ceiling.

"I had a car accident," he said. "Six months ago. I was driving to Melbourne from the island with my little sister, Olivia. There'd been another accident earlier. There was oil on the road. The car skidded…"

Elizabeth's hand tightened on his and he took a deep breath.

"We hit a tree, front left-hand side. The car…the car folded like a piece of freaking origami. I hit my head, passed out for a bit. Olivia—"

His throat closed as his sister's screams echoed in his head.

"You don't have to tell me. It's okay," Elizabeth said.

"I want to."

It took him a couple of shots at it. He held on to her hand for dear life as he told her how he'd woken and found Olivia pinned by twisted metal. How her face had been dark with blood, how icy her hand had been when he'd found it. How she'd whimpered and cried and begged. How he couldn't do anything, trapped beneath the steering wheel and the collapsed dash.

He stopped only when he got to the end. He couldn't make

himself say it. Couldn't explain how Olivia had pleaded with him to do something to stop the pain, right up until the moment she'd fallen silent and the desperate, labored rasp of her breathing had stopped, and how he'd held her hand until the rescue crew arrived and cut him free and forced him to relinquish his grip.

Elizabeth rolled onto her side and put her arms around him and held him tightly. Neither of them said anything for a long time. Then she lifted her face and pressed a kiss to his chin.

"I've sorry. Which is woefully inadequate, of course, and does nothing to change anything. But I'm sorry it happened, and I'm sorry your sister died. And I'm sorry you have to live with the memories. I can only imagine how hard that must be."

He hadn't told her because he wanted her pity or her sympathy or even her empathy. He'd told her because she deserved to understand why a grown man had hammered down her door and tried to lose himself in her arms last night.

And yet somehow, her calm, honest words soothed something inside him.

He pressed a kiss to her forehead, then her closed eyelids, then the end of her nose. She lifted her face and he found her mouth, returning the gentle pressure of her lips against his.

Slowly his offering of gratitude turned into something more needy and demanding. She shifted against him, her hips pressing against his thighs. His tongue slid into her mouth and stroked hers slowly, languorously. Her hand smoothed beneath his T-shirt to slide up onto his chest, her fingers shaping his pecs before skimming over his nipple.

He rolled toward her, pushing her silk robe out of the way. She arched her back as he lowered his head to pull a nipple into his mouth. Her hands found his shoulders and kneaded the muscles there as he suckled and teased and tasted her.

They pressed together, skin seeking skin, hardness seeking

softness. She tugged on the waistband of his boxer-briefs, releasing his hard-on. Then she lifted her leg over his hip and guided him into her wet heat. He gritted his teeth as his erection slid inside her.

She felt so good, so tight and good. He rocked his hips and she rocked with him. He cupped her breasts and teased her nipples and kissed her and kissed her. Her palms smoothed across his back, her fingers clenching into his skin with each slow, slippery thrust.

And then she was coming, throbbing around him as she gasped into his mouth and his own climax was washing through him like a tidal wave, relentless and all-conquering and undeniable.

He stayed inside her afterward, savoring the closeness. His eyes were very heavy and he closed them briefly.

She knew now. She knew everything. Pressing one last kiss to her cheek, he drifted into sleep.

ELIZABETH WAITED UNTIL HE was breathing steadily and slowly before pulling away from him. He frowned as she slipped free and she caressed his chest soothingly until he settled again.

She crossed to the bathroom and shut the door as quietly as possible. Then she sat on the closed toilet lid and pressed her face into her hands.

The horror of what he'd been through was almost impossible to comprehend. Being trapped with his sister yet unable to do anything as she died....

It was more than any person should have to bear. It was cruel and unlucky and hard. The stuff of nightmares.

For a moment Elizabeth teetered on the brink of crying, overwhelmed by his pain and grief. She breathed through her mouth in big gulps, pressing her fingertips against her closed eyelids, willing the tears away.

Slowly she got a grip on herself. Her losing it wasn't going to change anything. Nate didn't need her to beat her chest with anguish over his sad story. He was living with the aftermath of major trauma. Grappling with grief and guilt and anger and loss on a daily, perhaps hourly basis. He needed comfort and support and patience, not tears.

She let her hands fall into her lap, then she stood and went to the basin and ran the taps. She washed her face and patted it dry. With a bit of luck, Nate would still be asleep and she could climb back into bed with him.

It took a few seconds for her eyes to adjust to the dimmer light of the bedroom when she exited the bathroom, but the moment they did she saw what her instincts had already told her—the bed was empty.

Nate was gone.

She was surprised, and yet she wasn't. He was a man, with more than his fair share of pride. She'd heard the shame and self-laceration in his voice when he'd told his story. She bet he gave himself a hard time for every moment of weakness or doubt.

She sat for a moment, thinking. Just as they had yesterday, her instincts told her to go after Nate. But there was something she needed to do first. For both of them.

She showered and dressed and walked up the hill to the backpacker's lodge where she'd noticed a sign advertising an Internet café. She paid her money, then settled into a worn-out office chair in front of a worn-out computer and rested her fingers on the worn-out keyboard.

She wasted a few minutes logging in to check her e-mail account. There was a note from Violet there, full of apologies for "blabbing to D.D." about Elizabeth's whereabouts. Elizabeth sent a quick response, assuring her friend that she'd done the right thing. She explained that she and Martin had agreed to part as friends and started writing a description of the island

and the weather before she caught herself and realized she was stalling.

She deleted the travelogue, assured Violet that she'd write more soon and sent the e-mail. Then she called up a search engine and typed in *post-traumatic stress*. She hit enter and waited to see what Google would offer her.

Lots, was the answer. More than she could ever take in in a lifetime. She read for over three hours about the various symptoms and treatment of post-traumatic stress disorder. By the time she pushed the chair away from the desk she had as many questions as she did answers. Nate's drinking, his reliance on distraction, his avoidance of his business partner and retreat from his former life…it seemed to her that he must be suffering from a broad range of classic PTSD symptoms: reexperiencing the event in the form of flashbacks; avoiding places and events that might trigger one; hyperarousal or being on edge; problems with sleep and angry outbursts. But it was impossible for her to know without talking to him.

She made note of a few book titles and went to the bookstore five doors up to see what they had to offer. There was one self-help title that didn't look very promising, but she had more luck at the local library. By the end of the day she felt reasonably well-informed.

Well-informed enough to understand what she was getting into if she tried to pursue this thing with Nate.

It was clear that recovery was going to be long and slow, if it occurred at all. Some people never fully healed from the trauma that tore their lives apart. Like Nate, they retreated into a corner and survived as best they could. Many of them turned to alcohol and drugs.

It was a lot to take on. Which meant she had a decision to make. A big one.

She'd known Nathan Jones for five days, give or take a few hours either way. She didn't know what school he'd gone to or his parents' names or what his favorite color was or the name of his first pet. She didn't know which way he leaned politically or whether he gave to charity or which five people, living or dead, he'd invite to dinner.

What she did know was that he needed her. She knew that when he touched her she felt beautiful and sexy and brave. She knew he was kind and generous, despite the fact that his own life was overshadowed by tragedy and trauma.

And she knew that when he'd pressed his head to her chest and sobbed out his pain she'd wanted to take his burden away from him with a fierce, bone-deep urgency that defied logic and common sense.

So, it really wasn't a decision at all, when it came down to it.

Maybe she was crazy to feel this way after only five days. But she was sure stranger things had happened in the world. And at the end of the day, it was what it was. And what it was was this: she was invested. Heavily.

So.

Armed with her new knowledge, self and otherwise, she went searching for Nate.

NATE AVOIDED MAIN STREET for the next few days. Every time he thought about what he'd done—running crying to Elizabeth like a little kid and dumping all his ugly, messed-up shit on her in one foul swoop—he got angry with himself and life and fate all over again.

Apparently it wasn't enough that he'd lost his sister and his business and everything that had once made him feel complete and successful and alive. Apparently he had to throw the last remnants of his pride and self-respect on the table, too, and barter them away for a few moments of comfort and succor.

It was freaking humiliating. And what scared him the most

was how much he wanted to do it all over again. Talking to Lizzy, having her hold him and listen and understand, had been the most difficult and yet comforting few hours he'd experienced in months. For a short time, the constant tension binding his chest and shoulders had eased.

Which was why he had to stay away from Main Street and the Isle of Wight Hotel and anywhere Lizzy might be. They'd had sex a handful of times. He'd helped her out with her father, given her a sailing lesson and her first experience of oral sex. None of those things gave him the right to impose on her the way he had. He'd stepped over the line, way over the line. She'd been incredibly generous, listening to him, soothing him, but he already knew she was a good person. No way was he going to impose on her goodwill again and take advantage of her good nature. No. Way.

It didn't stop him from thinking about her all the time, of course. About the crisp, cool sound of her voice and the warm light in her eyes and the way she frowned when she didn't quite understand if he was joking or not.

Amazing that you could miss someone who had barely arrived in your life, and yet that was the way he felt. Just as well he was never going to see her again.

He killed the days with beer and surfing and sailing, and when that still left the night hours to fill he walked the beach, following the sand around the island until the rising tide forced him to turn back.

On the third day of his self-imposed Elizabeth ban, he looked up from rigging the main sail on the *Ducky* to find her walking across the beach toward him. She was wearing a pair of bright pink board shorts and a long-sleeved aqua lycra rash vest. White zinc covered her nose and cheeks and a floppy hat shaded her face.

She should have looked ridiculous but she didn't. Lust and

need and want hit him in the solar plexus and he fixed his gaze on the shackle he was tightening and hoped he didn't look as goddamned desperate as he felt.

"You're a hard man to track down," she said when she came to a halt beside the catamaran.

"I've been busy."

He fed the headboard into the mast and began pulling on the halyard to hoist the sail.

"I see."

He concentrated on the sail, making sure it was locked in place before wrapping the halyard around the mast cleat.

Maybe if he simply ignored her, she would go away. Then he wouldn't have to look at her and want her and remind himself of all the good reasons why whatever had been happening between them was done and why it had never had a future in the first place.

It was such a childish notion that he immediately rejected it. At the very least he owed her an apology for the other night and for leaving the way he had.

He cleared his throat and forced himself to look at her. "Listen. About the other night. I'm sorry for barging in on you like I did. I was out of line and too pissed to make much sense and it shouldn't have happened."

He waited for her to respond, but she simply stared at him for a long moment before reaching for one of the coils of rope on the trampoline.

"This is the one we thread through the pulleys on the boom, right?" she asked.

He didn't understand why she was here. What she wanted. Then the penny dropped and he got it: she felt sorry for him. Poor old Nate, crying out his pain and fear. Boo freaking hoo.

He reached out and tugged the coil of rope from her hands.

"You should go," he said tersely.

"Should I?" She snatched the rope back.

He frowned. "I said I was sorry, okay? There's nothing more to say and I don't need a social worker."

"If I was your social worker, Nathan Jones, I would be up in front of an ethics committee in a flash. Now, where does this rope go?"

When he didn't do anything except continue to frown at her, she began uncoiling the rope.

"Fine. I'll do it my way and you can fix it later."

She moved to where one of the clam cleats was fixed on the starboard hull and started feeding the rope through it. A strand of hair slid out of her hat as she worked, grazing her cheek before coming to rest in a curl over her breast.

He told himself to tell her to go away again. He didn't want her pity. He wasn't sure what he did want from her, but it certainly wasn't that.

She glanced up then and he looked straight into the deep blue of her eyes.

"You owe me another sailing lesson," she said.

It wasn't as simple as that, and they both knew it. But he didn't have the resolve to push her away a third time, which probably made him a weak bastard. But then that was nothing new, was it?

NATE BARELY SPOKE a word as they prepared the *Ducky* for sailing. He gave her instructions and took care to avoid touching her and only made eye contact when necessary. She took her cue from him and worked in silence until they were ready to co-opt some of the other club members into helping them carry the *Ducky* to the water. This time she lent her might to the effort, even though it was mostly token might since there was a man at each corner. Still, it was symbolic. She was here to participate.

She moved to the opposite side of the cat as Nate once they were in the shallows, guiding the boat into deeper water.

"Up you get," Nate said, and she scrambled onto the trampoline, water streaming from her legs.

He joined her a few seconds later and they concentrated on getting the boat out. She ducked when he told her to and shuffled from side to side as he tacked first one way then another. She took the tiller when he raised the jib, then followed his instructions to reset it each time they tacked.

Slowly, over first one hour then two, the taut, distant expression left his face. Then and only then did she stretch out full length on the trampoline and rest her head on his thigh as he sat at the tiller, closing her eyes and crossing her ankles. She felt him look down at her but she didn't open her eyes. The tense thigh beneath her head slowly relaxed. After a few minutes, she turned her head and pressed a kiss against his skin.

"Lizzy..." he said. His voice was very low.

"Yes?"

"This isn't going to happen."

"Why not?"

He swore under his breath. "You know why not."

"No, Nathan, I don't." She sat up and turned to face him.

He was frowning again, and the taut look was back on his face.

"I don't want your pity, Elizabeth."

Amazing how unfriendly her own name sounded coming from him when she'd gotten so used to the way he called her Lizzy.

"Just as well, because you don't have my pity. You are the least pitiful person I know, as a matter of fact. I *empathize* with you. I feel for you. I regret your pain. But I don't pity you, Nathan. And if you don't understand the difference then maybe you should think about cutting back on all that beer you drink."

"I don't want your empathy, either." He sounded as sulky and out of sorts as a child but she understood that his weakness the other night struck at the heart of how he saw himself in the world.

"What do you want? My vagina? My breasts? My mouth? Am I leaving out any other useful body parts?"

He glared at her. "You came looking for me. Remember?"

"And you came looking for me the other night," she countered.

He looked away. "That was a mistake."

"Nathan…"

Because she didn't know what else to do, how to get through to him, she grabbed a fistful of his hair and pressed her mouth to his. He resisted her kiss at first, then his mouth opened beneath hers and his tongue slid into her mouth. She kissed him until they were both breathless. When they drew apart, he stared straight into her eyes and she saw so much desperation and need in him it made her chest ache.

"You don't understand," he said. "The other night—that's just the tip of the iceberg."

She nodded and raised her hand, counting off the points she'd researched. "Let me guess—flashbacks, night sweats, anxiety attacks, insomnia, quick to anger. How am I doing?"

A muscle tensed in his jaw. "I can't drive."

It was her turn to frown as she thought over all their time together. Sure enough, they'd walked everywhere.

"I take it you've tried?" she asked after a brief silence.

"Yes."

"Do you mind being in a car when someone else is driving?" she asked.

He brushed a hand over his hair and squinted toward the horizon. He clearly hated talking about this stuff, was about as comfortable as a cat having its fur stroked the wrong way.

"I tolerate it," he said. "It's not my favorite thing in the world, but I can do it. But I don't like driving at night."

She nodded. "Okay."

He glanced across at her. "That's it?"

She shrugged. "It's good to know these things."

"Lizzy."

"You keep saying that," she said. Then she leaned close and laid her cheek against his. "I like you, Nathan Jones. You make me laugh and you challenge me and you're very, very good in bed. I want to keep spending time with you. What's so hard about any of that?"

"I'm a basket case, Lizzy."

"I'm not exactly a bargain myself, you know. I've spent my entire adult life pleasing other people. I'm fresh out of an engagement I never should have agreed to in the first place. Before I met you I'd never had sex in any position other than missionary."

His gaze searched hers and she held his gaze unflinchingly.

"You should be running for the hills," he said.

"But I'm not."

He reached out and framed her face with his hands. "If I was a better person, I'd make you run."

"You could try. There's no guarantee you'd succeed, though. I've discovered a stubborn streak lately."

"Lizzy."

"There you go again with the Lizzy-ing." Then, because she could see how much this small moment of connection meant to him, how much he needed it, and she was very afraid that any minute the emotion welling up inside her was going to translate into waterworks, she leaned close and kissed him again.

THAT NIGHT, NATE TURNED away from rinsing the last of their dinner plates at the sink to find Elizabeth absorbed in the local paper at the kitchen table.

The overhead light shone in her pale blond hair and cast shadows beneath her cheekbones. He stood at the counter, folded the tea towel and resisted the urge to go to her and make love to her for the third time that day.

She was beautiful and funny and generous and prim— and he couldn't believe she was here. Couldn't believe that she hadn't backed off at a million miles an hour after his performance the other night or the revelation that he was still so haunted by the accident that he couldn't do something as simple and everyday as drive a car.

But she hadn't flinched, hadn't so much as looked away when he'd confessed his weakness. And when they'd come back to his place after sailing, she'd pushed him down onto the bed and left him in no doubt as to whether she still wanted him, despite everything.

Lying in bed with her in his arms, he'd caught a glimpse of a future that might not be simple, bare-bones, batten-down-the-hatches survival. A future that wasn't simply about endurance.

He walked around the counter and rested his hand on the back of her chair.

"Having a nice time there?" he said.

She glanced over her shoulder at him. "Did you know they delivered twin wombats at the local wildlife reserve? There's a picture here but they said they're not letting anyone in to see them until they're fully weaned. Look how cute they are."

He dutifully scanned the photograph accompanying the story. "Cute."

"We don't have wombats in England," she said. "The closest we have are the Wombles of Wimbledon Common."

She was being funny and he rewarded her with a kiss. "Want to toast marshmallows on what's left of the fire in the barbecue?" he asked.

"Why, sir, I thought you'd never ask."

They lay on the picnic blanket and made themselves sick and sticky with gooey marshmallows.

"I never know when to stop," Elizabeth said as she rubbed her stomach. "My mother used to call me a pelican—eyes too big for my belly-can."

"You miss her."

She pulled a face. "Stupid, huh? She's been gone for more than twenty years."

"Not stupid," he said. Impossible to stop his thoughts from going to Olivia. There were so many things he missed about her. The sound of her off-key singing when she danced to her iPod, her shoes cluttering the front hallway thanks to her habit of kicking them off the moment she entered the house, the way she'd send him little text messages through the day— their own personal Twitter—keeping him up-to-date on her world.

"You never mention your parents," Elizabeth said.

It took him a moment to change gears, push Olivia deep inside himself.

"They're both dead. Dad had a car accident when I was ten. Mum died a few years ago. Cancer."

"I'm so sorry."

"Yeah. We're not exactly the lucky Joneses, are we?" he said.

She shifted beside him, rolling onto her side and propping her head on her bent arm. "It must have made it harder. Losing

Olivia, I mean. Because you were her parent for the past few years."

For longer than that. His mother had battled for nearly two years before dying. Olivia had come to live with him when she was twelve. He'd had five years of being her everything before she died.

He'd been silent too long and Elizabeth reached out to touch his chest.

"You don't like to talk about it."

"Not much to say, is there?"

She leaned close and kissed him. "No, I guess there isn't."

She settled down beside him again, her head on his shoulder this time, her arm across his chest. She didn't say anything else, and neither did he.

He made love to her when they turned in for the night, swallowing her moans as he pushed himself deep inside her. She wrapped her legs around his waist and dug her fingers into his back as she came, her body strung as tight as a bow. He hung on to the pleasure for as long as he could before he succumbed. Then he tucked her body against his own and fell asleep.

9

NATE WOKE WITH AN idea fully formed in his mind the next morning. He wanted to give Elizabeth something back, something in return for her thoughtful silences and silken body and warm eyes. Something to make her smile.

He eased out of bed to find his phone and slipped outside to make a couple of calls.

Elizabeth was sitting up and blinking by the time he returned.

"No sailing today. I've got a surprise," he said.

"What have you been up to?" she asked suspiciously.

"Come on. Out of bed and into the shower. We've got places to go, people to see."

"Nathan. What's going on?"

"It's a surprise."

"What kind of a surprise?"

She looked so adorable, with her mussed hair and faintly imperious frown. He ducked his head to kiss her before responding.

"The kind of surprise that's a surprise."

She was even more curious when he walked into town with her to collect her car.

He could feel her looking at him as he buckled his seat belt, knew what she was thinking. It was the first time he'd driven with her, and she had to be wondering how he'd cope.

"I'll be fine, don't worry," he said.

It would have been true, too, if a car full of teenage surfers hadn't blown through an intersection on the way out of town. Elizabeth braked sharply and they both jerked forward in their seats. The strap bit into his chest and he lifted his hands instinctively to shield his face.

"God. I'm so sorry. He came out of nowhere," Elizabeth said.

She was pale from shock and Nate tried to find the words to reassure her but there was something in his throat and he couldn't seem to breathe around it.

Not now. Don't you do this to me. Don't you dare freaking do this to me.

But his stupid, messed-up subconscious was off and running, running a highlights reel from the night of the accident. Cold adrenaline swept through him as the car pulled over to the curb. He heard the sound of a car door opening and closing. Then Elizabeth was unbuckling his seat belt and pulling him out of the car.

"Sit. Put your head between your legs," she said, pushing him onto the grass at the side of the road.

He had no choice but to comply, sitting with his legs drawn up, his head hanging between his knees as he concentrated on slowing his breathing. In, out. In, out. After what felt like an age the shaking stopped. He opened his eyes and stared at the grass between his feet.

Shit.

Shit, shit, shit, shit.

He'd organized something fun for her, then screwed it up with his bullshit. A simple drive out of town, no big deal, and he'd turned it into a three-ring circus.

The futility of what they were doing—what he'd been

fooling himself they were doing—hit him. This was never going to work. He was a selfish prick for even trying to keep her by his side.

A warm hand landed in the center of his back.

"How are you doing?"

He was so frustrated, so freaking over it, he could barely stand to have her touch him. Especially when he knew how he must appear right now, hunched over on the side of the road like the basket case he was.

"I'm good," he said between gritted teeth.

"I wish I'd got their license plate number. Horrible little oiks. I'd love to send a note to their parents. I'm sure they'd be thrilled to know their children were driving around like maniacs."

Not quite what he'd expected her to say. But Elizabeth was always surprising him. He risked a glance at her. She was watching him, a question in her eyes.

There was no pity there. No contempt or regret or embarrassment.

It occurred to him that he was one lucky bastard to have opened the door to Elizabeth Mason just over a week ago. Possibly the luckiest bastard on the planet.

"Would this note be on monogrammed stationery?" he asked after a long silence. "I'm assuming you have some."

"Of course. But unfortunately I didn't bring it with me. So I'd have to make do with some from the Isle of Wight."

"Yes. That would definitely get their attention—a stern reprimand on letterhead from the local pub."

She smiled and gave a little shrug.

She was so damned gorgeous and sweet and funny....

She stood and dusted off the seat of her pants.

"It's not a bad idea, you know—writing a note to their parents. You'd be surprised how many big, bad boys are still afraid of their mothers."

He pushed himself to his feet.

"Come on. We'll go home and you can give me some sailing pointers," she said.

The thought of going home and disappearing inside his bubble of Elizabeth and beer and sun and silence seemed pretty good with the last of the adrenaline still making itself felt in his body.

But he'd been walking backward for so long. Retreating, retreating, retreating. No way was he going to cap the whole cowering-by-the-side-of-the-road thing by running home with his tail between his legs.

And he wanted to do this for Elizabeth.

"I'm not ready to go home yet," he said.

Elizabeth eyed him steadily. "You can surprise me another day, you know. If that's what it's about."

He gestured toward the car. "Let's go."

She hesitated a moment, then she walked around to the driver's side door. Nate stepped toward the open passenger door. He kept his gaze fixed on the seat in front of him, but it was impossible to stop the tension that banded his chest and choked his throat.

But he knew he could do this. He'd done it before, after the accident. He'd allowed people to drive him around, back and forth to doctors and consultants. To Olivia's funeral. To the office. He hadn't liked it, but he'd done it. And he'd finally gotten used to it, eventually.

So. It would be bad when he first got in. But it would get better. It would.

He took a couple of deep belly breaths, then slid into the car. His immediate impulse was to get the hell out. It was too small, too closed in. And once the car started moving, there'd be the speed to deal with, the world rushing up at him....

He closed his hand around the seat belt clasp and pulled the belt across his chest. He clicked it in place, then gripped the fastener as tightly as he could. Just to know that he could release the belt any time he wanted.

Elizabeth put on her own belt and started the car. She signaled to pull onto the road, but didn't make any move to shift the car in gear or release the hand brake.

"We don't have to do this," she said.

"Yeah, we do."

She didn't say anything else, simply put the car in gear, released the handbrake and pulled out onto the road. A wash of anxiety rushed through Nate's body, the instinctive desire to escape something that terrified him. He kept breathing into his belly, the way his therapist had taught him, and slowly his heart rate slowed and the hectic, swirling chatter in his mind settled.

He loosened his grip on the seat belt, then deliberately relaxed the muscles in his shoulders. Finally he focused on the road ahead.

"We need to turn right up ahead," he said. "I'll tell you when."

"Okay." She glanced across at him. "Would it help if I sang?"

"Are you any good?"

"No."

He smiled. "Sure. Why not?"

She thought for a moment, then started singing "God Save the Queen." She hadn't been lying—she had a terrible singing voice. When she'd finished the British national anthem, she moved on to Abba.

By the time the turnoff came into view his hands were loose in his lap and most of the tension was gone.

"Right here," he said.

She nodded and turned and he gave her directions the rest of the way. Soon they were pulling into the parking lot of the Phillip Island Wildlife Park. She read the sign, then spun toward him with a hopeful smile.

"This is the place where they have the baby wombats."

He put on his best poker face. "Is it?"

"Nate…"

"Patience is a virtue. Surely your grandmother taught you that one?"

She poked her tongue out at him but followed him inside the administration building. The head ranger, Henry, came to the ticket booth when Nate gave his name to the cashier. They all shook hands and the older man led them into the park and along a dusty dirt track.

"This isn't the usual tour, is it?" Elizabeth asked after a few minutes.

"I'm not sure," Nate lied.

She nudged him with her elbow. "Is he taking us to see the baby wombats or not?"

"You're the kind of kid who used to snoop around under the Christmas tree, feeling up her presents, aren't you?"

"Yes."

She looked so hopeful that he couldn't help laughing. He slid his arm around her shoulder.

"Relax, Lizzy. All will be revealed."

It took them five minutes to reach the wombat enclosure. Henry paused before letting them inside.

"These joeys are six months old and they're still in the pouch. They won't leave permanently for another two to four months, but they come out regularly to look around. Be warned—their claws are long and strong, even though they're only babies."

Elizabeth nodded her understanding and followed him into the enclosure. Nate stood to one side and watched her face as Henry delivered a small, hairy bundle into her arms.

A slow, incredulous smile curled her mouth and her eyes

lit with pleasure. "Oh. He's beautiful! Nate, look at him, isn't he adorable? Or is it a she?"

"They're both boys," Henry said.

"He's so soft." She ran her hands over his fur, then she glanced across at Nate, inviting him to share her pleasure.

Their eyes met and held and for a few precious seconds there was nothing else in the world. Then Henry brought over the second wombat and the moment was gone.

They spent fifteen minutes in the enclosure and Elizabeth was able to nurse both the baby wombats as well as pat their mother.

She caught his hand once they had left the park, forcing him to stop.

"Thank you. I don't know how you arranged for that to happen, but it was wonderful. Just…wonderful."

He shrugged, embarrassed by her gratitude. "Smartsell donated some money to the park's on-site hospital building fund last year. I made a phone call or two. It was no big deal."

"It was to me." She stood on tiptoes and kissed him.

He smiled. Couldn't help himself. He'd wanted to give her something, a small moment of pleasure, and he had.

Later that night, he rolled her onto her knees and took her from behind, the way he knew she liked it. She rocked her hips and cried out when she came, then he grit his teeth and hung on and made it happen all over again before he let himself lose control. When they were both lying limp and breathless afterward, he ran his fingers through her hair and tried to remember what it was like before she came into his life.

He couldn't. Probably because he didn't want to. She made everything better. Her smile, her laughter—God, he loved to make her laugh. He also loved the way she shivered when he touched her, and the way she was simply there when his stuff got on top of him, how she looked at him so calmly, not judging, before saying something incredibly prosaic and everyday and grounding.…

She was smart and practical and generous and bloody brave. And she was in his arms, right now. In his life. It was almost too good to be true.

"You should give up your room at the pub, move in here," he said, before he had a chance to second-guess himself.

He felt her body tense in his arms, then she lifted her head so she could look into his face. They stared into each other's eyes for a long moment, then she returned her head to his chest.

"Okay."

He waited for her to say more, but she didn't.

"We can move into the main house, if you'd prefer it," he said.

She lifted her head to look at him again. "What about my father? Wouldn't he want to have a say in that…?"

Nate shrugged. "There are two bedrooms. He offered to move into the studio when I first came down to the island, but I didn't much care where I was."

She frowned, then her brow cleared. "This is your place, isn't it? God, I'm so dense sometimes. All this time, I thought you were renting from my father, but it's the other way around, isn't it?"

"I bought this place to renovate it. Was going to do something big and modern like the place next door."

She wrinkled her nose and he laughed.

"Maybe you should take a look inside before you pass judgment. It's pretty nice over there. Imported stone floors. Teak woodwork. State-of-the-art everything."

"And absolutely no charm or character, I bet. No, thank you. I'll take these four walls and two windows and wooden floor over that perfect place every time. *Every time.*"

He was silent for a moment. "So I take it that's a no to moving into the main house?"

"Correct."

She returned her head to his chest and he resumed combing his fingers through her hair.

She was moving in. He knew it was only temporary, until Sam returned from the Sydney-to-Hobart race. Knew that she had no solid plans for what might happen after she met her father, and that her life was elsewhere, about as far from Nate's very circumscribed world here on the island as it was possible to be...

But for now, she was staying. That was more than enough for a guy who had turned taking it day-by-day into an art form.

IT TOOK ELIZABETH ALL OF twenty minutes to move out of the pub and into Nate's place the next day: she packed her bag, paid her bill then drove the rental to his house and parked in the drive.

There wasn't a single doubt in her mind that she was doing the right thing as she dragged her suitcase from the trunk of the car. Whatever it was that was happening between her and Nate, it felt right. This place, right now, was exactly where she wanted and needed to be.

When she entered the studio, Nate was shoving a huge old wardrobe into the corner.

"Where did that come from?" she asked.

"Spare room. Thought you'd want somewhere to put your things."

"Ah. Other than on the floor or the bed, you mean?"

Then she glanced around and realized he'd cleaned up. Even the bed was freshly made.

"Dear me. Don't you think it's dangerous to set standards

that may never be met again?" she asked, absurdly touched
that he'd gone to so much trouble for her.

"It's all downhill from here, baby," he said, but he was
smiling.

"I guess I'd better unpack, then."

He helped her, then they walked to the yacht club and
took the *Ducky* out for the afternoon, gliding across the deep
blue ocean, the salt spray on their faces and the wind in their
hair.

It became a routine of sorts over the next week—whatever
needed to be done was tackled in the morning, then they went
sailing or Nate surfed while she paddled in the shallows and
watched him defy Mother Nature and gravity all at once.

Twice the postman delivered fat envelopes from Smartsell.
Nate barely glanced at them before adding them to the pile in
the corner. She didn't say a word. One day, he'd want to pick
up the threads of his old life, but clearly he wasn't ready yet.
So be it.

After much deliberation, she made contact with her grandparents for the first time after arriving in Australia. She and
her grandfather exchanged a few very polite words about
the weather and her grandmother's health before Elizabeth
told him about Sam being interstate and that she most likely
wouldn't be home for Christmas because she was waiting for
him to return to the Island. There was a short pause and she
pictured her grandfather's face, knew that he was probably
aching to tell her what a mistake she was making, what a huge
mistake she'd already made by ending things with Martin.

"Well. We'll miss you, of course. But if this is something
you feel you have to do…"

"It is."

"Then we both wish you the best of luck, Elizabeth," her
grandfather said.

It was hard to stay angry when she could hear the sadness

in his voice. They talked for a few more minutes before ending the call and afterward she went for a long walk along the beach to clear her head.

When she returned to London, she was going to insist that they all sit down and talk honestly, adult to adult, for perhaps the first time in her life. Perhaps then they would all have a better understanding of one another.

A WEEK TO THE DAY after Elizabeth had moved in with Nate, they arrived home from an afternoon out on the *Ducky* to find a beaten-up four-wheel drive parked behind her car in the driveway.

"Looks like you've got a visitor," she said.

She glanced at Nate, but he was frowning.

"Who is it?" she asked.

He threw her an unreadable look. "That's Sam's car."

She stilled. Sam. As in Sam Blackwell. Her father.

"I thought he wasn't due back until after the New Year?"

It was only the fifteenth. She hadn't even begun to think about coming face-to-face with him yet. Hadn't even begun to think about what she wanted to say to him, what she wanted to ask.

"He wasn't."

Nate took her hand and gave it a squeeze. "You okay?"

She thought about it for a second, then nodded. "Yes. I mean, I have to meet him sometime, don't I?"

They walked down the driveway and past the house. The rear door was open, the bead curtain swinging in the breeze. The radio was on in the kitchen and she could see someone moving around inside. Her father.

Nate walked toward the back steps but she resisted his lead. He stopped and looked at her.

"You want a moment?"

She nodded, appreciating his understanding. He didn't say

anything else, simply squeezed her hand one last time before releasing it and climbing the steps to the house.

Elizabeth pressed her palm flat against her churning stomach as he disappeared inside.

Her father. She was about to meet her father. Unexpectedly, despite the fact that she'd been waiting for him for more than two weeks now. She wanted so much from this meeting. She wanted to have a father again. She wanted to belong to someone.

It was a hell of a lot of expectation to bring to a first meeting, but there wasn't much she could do about that.

She could hear conversation inside the house. She took a deep breath, let it out, then climbed the back steps.

The bead curtain announced her arrival and two heads turned toward her as she stopped just inside the door. A nervous smile curled her mouth as she stared at the very tanned, fit-looking man leaning against the kitchen counter. His hair was cropped short and mottled with gray, and he was dressed neatly in a pair of dark navy tracksuit pants and a polo shirt. His eyes seemed very blue against his dark skin as he looked at her, the lines around his eyes and mouth deeply scored. She tried to find some point of resemblance between them. The eye color, perhaps—although her mother had been blue-eyed, too. Maybe the shape of her chin? And perhaps her high forehead…?

She took a tentative step forward. "Hello. Um, I'm Elizabeth."

He nodded. "Sam."

He'd been studying her, too, and she waited for him to say something else, ready to take her cue from him. But he didn't say anything. Instead, he turned to Nathan and resumed their interrupted conversation.

"Anyway, they reckon it'll take weeks just for the swelling

to go down, let alone for them to work out if they can operate or not. Bloody doctors."

Elizabeth stared at his profile, utterly thrown. She hadn't expected her father to throw his arms around her and hold her to his bosom or anything as dramatic as that, but she'd expected *something*. Some recognition that she was more than a casual acquaintance.

Across the room, Nate was frowning, his gaze going from her to Sam and back again.

"Sam was just telling me that he's torn a ligament in his knee. Which is why he's home early," he said.

For the first time Elizabeth noticed the crutches propped in the corner and the bulge around her father's left knee beneath his tracksuit pants.

"That must have been very disappointing for you. I know you were looking forward to the race," she said.

Sam glanced at her briefly before looking away again. "*Disappointing* isn't the word. I'm going to miss all the majors this season now, on top of losing a major charter to the Caribbean. I'll be stuck on these bloody things for months." He thumped the crutches with a fist.

She tried to think of something else to say, but her mind was a complete blank. "Well. That's disappointing," she said again.

Her father shrugged impatiently and reached for his crutches.

"Better go unpack." His gaze took in the plates in the sink and the newspaper Nate had left folded on the kitchen table. "Looks like there's plenty of work to do around here, anyway."

He tucked the crutches under his arms and started down the hallway.

Elizabeth stared at his retreating back for a long beat. Then she swiveled on her heel and headed for the door. She barreled down the stairs and across the yard and didn't stop until she was in the studio. Then she simply stood, hands loose by her sides, and tried to understand what had happened.

She'd just met her father for the first time. They'd introduced themselves. And then he had proceeded to ignore her.

"You okay?" Nate's warm hands landed on her shoulders, his thumbs brushing the nape of her neck.

"I just— I thought—" She shook her head, unable to articulate the jumble of hurt, outrage, anger and disappointment churning inside her.

Nate slid an arm around her, his forearm beneath her breasts as he pulled her against him. He pressed a kiss into her hair and laid his cheek against her head. His silent support helped calm her thoughts and finally she faced the reluctant truth.

"This isn't going to be what I want it to be, is it?"

Nate pulled her tighter against his body. "Give it time."

"Nate. The man is not interested. Never has been."

"It's not about you, Lizzy. He doesn't even know you. Whatever is going on is Sam's problem. He's always been more happy on his own than with anyone else. That's why he looks after this place for me. In the off season, there are only about seven thousand people on the island, and he likes it that way."

She understood what he was saying but it felt like a cruel joke to have found a parent only to learn that he wanted nothing to do with her.

"Want to walk into town and buy some fresh fish for dinner?" Nate asked.

She nodded, unable to speak past the emotion choking her throat. He turned her around in his arms and tilted her chin so she was forced to meet his gaze.

"It's his loss, Lizzy. Believe me."

There was so much warmth in his eyes. It went a long way to assuaging her hurts. She reached out to touch his face. He was such a good person. It continually amazed her that in the midst of all the crap he was dealing with he found room to care for others.

For a long moment she battled with the urge to say the things that were in her heart. It was too soon, her gut told her. But one day she wouldn't bite her tongue. One day she would tell this wonderful, wounded, generous man how she felt about him.

She dropped her hand.

"Let's go."

NATE HELD HIS TONGUE ALL afternoon and well into the evening. He watched Sam sit silently through a meal of fish and grilled prawns and salad, never once asking Elizabeth about her life, her teaching, her dreams, her past, and told himself that it was Sam's problem and not Nate's place to interfere. He'd never been the kind of person who stuck his nose into other people's business. It simply wasn't his style. He dealt with his crap and he let other people deal with theirs, a mindset that had only become more entrenched since the accident. He didn't want people offering him unsolicited advice, getting in his face, and he extended the same courtesy to others.

But listening to Elizabeth make polite conversation with her father over dinner, watching her take Sam's indifference on the chin again and again as Sam offered monosyllables and shrugs and avoided eye contact made Nate want to hurt something. Preferably Sam.

Not surprisingly, Sam made an excuse about catching up on his sleep after dinner and disappeared to his room. There was a small silence, then Elizabeth turned to Nate with a bright smile.

"Want to toast marshmallows on the barbecue again?"

That brave, bright smile pretty much tore it for him.

"Sure. Why don't you get a head start and I'll be out in a tick?" he said easily.

"Okay. But remember, he who snoozes loses."

"Sure. I won't be long."

What he had in mind would take about sixty seconds—he figured that was about how long it would take for him to grab Sam by the scruff of the neck and shake some sense into him.

Nate waited until Elizabeth had gone outside before walking to Sam's bedroom. The door was slightly ajar and he knocked on the door frame and waited, temper simmering.

"Who is it?" Sam asked.

Nate pushed the door open. Sam was sitting on the edge of the bed, his bad leg extended in front of him. He'd stripped to his boxer shorts and polo shirt and for the first time in all the years Nate had known him he looked older than his fifty-two years.

"What the hell is wrong with you?" Nate demanded.

"Just leave it, mate."

"No, *mate,* I won't. She's your daughter. Have a conversation with her. Get to know her."

"It's not that simple."

"Yeah, it is. It's really simple."

"Look, I know you're only looking out for her, but it's best this way. I just spoke to a mate up in Melbourne, he's going to let me bunk down with him for a few weeks."

"So, what? You're just going to head off tomorrow? You're giving her *one night?* When she's flown halfway around the world to find you?"

Sam didn't say anything.

"You're an asshole, you know that?" Nate said. "A selfish asshole."

Sam's mouth tightened and he pushed himself awkwardly to his feet. "You finished? Had your say?"

He hobbled forward, trying to crowd Nate out of the room.

Nate jabbed a finger at him. "If you do this, if you take off tomorrow, you're the biggest pussy I know."

"That'd sting a whole lot more if it didn't come from a guy who's been hiding in the bottom of a beer bottle for the past four months."

Nate flinched.

"What's wrong? You can dish it out but you can't take it?" Sam said. "Don't come in here on your high moral horse, telling me what to do and how to behave when you don't even have the balls to open *your own bloody mail.*"

The other man's face was red and a vein pulsed at his neck.

"If you go, don't bother coming back," Nate said.

He turned and walked away. The door slammed behind him, the sound echoing up the hallway. Nate strode into the kitchen and swore viciously. He really, really wanted to punch something. His hand curled into a fist and he tensed, ready to smack a hole in one of the overhead kitchen cabinets. Then he remembered Elizabeth was outside, waiting for him.

He didn't want her to know what had gone down. Didn't want her to know he'd had to threaten her father to try and make the guy stick around.

He let his breath hiss between his teeth and braced his hands on the counter, dropping his head and taking a few seconds to let the anger drain out of him. If Sam went ahead with his plan and bailed on Elizabeth tomorrow... Nate was going to be sorely pressed not to punch his lights out.

He lifted his head and released his grip on the counter. He would deal with whatever came tomorrow when it happened. Right now, Elizabeth was waiting for him.

He turned toward the door but his gaze snagged on the pile of envelopes overflowing from the magazine rack in the corner.

For a moment he stood frozen. Then he brushed a hand over his head.

Bloody Sam.

Annoyed all over again, he grabbed a couple of beers from the fridge and took them outside. Elizabeth looked up from toasting a stick full of marshmallows as he exited the house.

"Everything okay?" she asked.

"Yeah. Why wouldn't it be?" he said, even though he could hear the edge in his own voice.

"You're frowning, for starters."

She paused, waiting, and when he didn't say anything she cocked her head to one side. "Going to play it strong and silent on me, huh?"

"Silent, anyway."

He sat on the picnic blanket and she held the stick out to him.

"Have a marshmallow, then."

It was one of the things he loved about her the most, the calm way she had of simply accepting things the way they were. She never pushed. She never clung or offered advice he hadn't asked for or tried to tell him what to do or how to be.

He slid a marshmallow off the gooey stick and put it in his mouth. It tasted like burned sugar and she laughed when he pulled a face.

"Not my best batch."

He caught her hand and pulled her down onto the blanket.

"You okay?" he asked.

Her smile faded a little. "I'll survive."

He fought a battle with his conscience as he looked into

her eyes. Was it better to warn her or not? If Sam chose to go tomorrow, there was no way she could fail to take it as a kick in the teeth. But if he warned her in advance and Sam didn't wind up going, he would have upset her for nothing.

"You're frowning again."

She reached out and pressed her fingers against his forehead.

"Sam's talking about heading up to Melbourne tomorrow."

Her gaze dropped to the blanket. He reached for her hand and squeezed it. Still she didn't say anything and he used their joined hands to pull her into his lap. He wrapped his arms around her and she pressed her face into his neck.

They sat in the dark, the fire dying to embers, not saying a word for a long time.

10

ELIZABETH'S FATHER packed up his car and left the next morning. He had an excuse for his departure—a friend who wanted his advice on buying a boat. She listened to his thin explanation, then walked away without a word. A few weeks ago she would have smiled and waved and done her bit to smooth things over to keep the peace. For good or for ill, she wasn't that woman anymore. She wasn't going to deny herself or pretend anymore. Her father had made his decision, which was his right, just as it was her right to feel the way she felt in response. So be it.

She channeled her disappointment into cleaning the house, giving the kitchen and bathroom and living room a thorough going-over. Nate watched her wield the vacuum cleaner for a few minutes before wisely stepping away and leaving her to it. She cleaned out the fridge and wiped down the stove and scoured the sink and slowly, slowly let go of the tight, hurt feeling inside her.

Her father had rejected her. There. She'd admitted it. It wasn't a matter of simple disinterest. He didn't want to know her.

Stupid to pretend it didn't hurt—of course it did. But at least Nate had warned her last night and she'd had the chance to prepare herself. She'd lain awake in his arms, hoping against hope that Sam would choose to stay.

So much for hope.

She moved on to clearing the kitchen table, discarding yesterday's paper, culling a black banana from the fruit bowl, returning the salt and paper shakers to the cupboard. Her gaze fell on the pile of Nate's unopened mail and she drew the magazine rack toward herself and began to pile the envelopes together. Even if Nate was never going to open them there was no need for them to remain an eyesore.

He entered the kitchen as she finished stacking the envelopes into two neat piles.

"Hi. Where do you want these?" she asked, lifting her hair off the back of her neck. It was heading toward the hottest part of the day and the house was stuffy and warm.

Nate glanced at the envelopes. "They're fine where they are."

"I could help you go through them, if you like? Just in case there's anything you need to worry about."

"There isn't."

She hesitated a moment, then nodded. "All right."

She grabbed the first stack and knelt beside the magazine rack.

"Wait. Give them to me. I'll toss them," Nate said suddenly.

She looked up at him, surprised, but he was already scooping up the pile from the table. Wordlessly she handed over the remainder and watched as he walked out the back door.

She glanced at the empty magazine rack, feeling uneasy. Perhaps she should have left that particular sleeping dog lie. It was so hard to know what to do. She understood that Nate had worked out a strategy for himself over the past four months. He had his routines, his coping mechanisms. Who was she to push or pull him in another direction? Given what had happened to him, how it haunted him, it seemed to her that he was entitled to whatever peace he could find.

But she was also aware that it wasn't a long-term solution. She wanted more for him than this circumscribed life.

She sighed heavily and pushed herself to her feet. If he wanted to throw away his Smartsell paperwork, then it was up to him. She only hoped that one day, one of the letters would arrive and he'd feel an itch to open it.

NATE WALKED AROUND THE side of the house and dumped the armful of envelopes in the recycle bin. Something he should have been doing right from the start. Why the hell Jarvie felt the need to keep him in the loop he had no idea.

Okay. That was a lie. He knew why—Jarvie wanted him to come back. He hoped to entice Nate back to Melbourne and into the office with dispatches from the front line.

It wasn't going to work. Jarvie was going to have to live with things the way they were. Nate was now a silent partner. It was better for everyone that way.

Because he knew it had been a crappy day for Elizabeth, Nate rang her English friends, Lexie and Ross, and the four of them went out for dinner. He listened to her talk and laugh, watched the play of light over her face and the way she tilted her head when she was listening to something that engaged her.

Sam was a jerk for bailing on her.

It hit him during dessert that there was nothing holding Elizabeth in Australia anymore. With Sam gone, there was no reason for her to stay. Christmas was a few days away—it only made sense for her to return home to spend it with her grandparents and her friends.

He twisted his wineglass on the table.

He didn't want her to go.

He didn't want to contemplate what his life would be

without her. Couldn't even imagine trying to get through the night without her in his arms. But his need was not even close to being enough of a reason to ask Elizabeth to stay. He'd chosen to live this way—she had not. She had a life in London. A career as a teacher. Grandparents and friends.

Despite his best intentions, ways and means to bind her to his side raced through his mind. They could move into the main house. They could renovate, in whatever style or way Elizabeth dictated. Money wasn't an issue, after all. She wouldn't have to work if she didn't want to. He could give her anything—anything—that her heart desired.

He swallowed the last of his wine.

He wasn't going to do any of those things. No matter how much he wanted to.

He loved her too much to trap her.

He allowed the knowledge to wash over him. Of course he loved Lizzy. She was smart and kind and generous. She drove him wild in bed. She amused him endlessly. She made him wish he could turn back time. Six months ago, he would have pursued her and made her his. He would have done whatever it took to make her happy.

But he wasn't that man anymore. He couldn't drive. Until recently he couldn't get through the night without waking at least once, bathed in sweat, Olivia's screams in his head. He was no good to anyone. Fine for a holiday fling, but a liability in the long term.

The knowledge sat like a rock on his chest for the rest of the evening.

"You know, I don't think I even knew what summer was until I came here," Elizabeth said as they walked home along the beach. The wind blew her hair across her face and she caught the length of it in her hand and draped it over one shoulder. "It's hard to believe that it's probably snowing back home."

They turned onto the track to his street and he waited for her to toe on her sandals before they walked the short distance to his house.

Elizabeth flicked a glance at the steel-and-glass showpiece next door and shuddered theatrically.

"Promise me you won't ever build one of those," she said.

He looked at her, her hair silver, her eyes a very dark blue in the moonlight. "I promise."

"You want to lie on the blanket and watch the stars?"

"No."

A slow smile curled her mouth. "Really. What did you have in mind?"

He showed her, leading her to the studio and peeling her clothes off slowly. Kissing the tan lines on her shoulders and breasts. Pushing her back onto the bed and taking her nipple into his mouth. She moaned her pleasure and spread her legs languorously. He licked and sucked and nibbled his way down her belly, smiling when her breath caught as she understood where he was going.

He loved the way she responded to his touch. So openly, so unashamedly. Despite her very proper accent and her perfect manners and her very practical nature, in bed she was a willing, greedy wanton and he loved it.

He hooked his thumbs into the waistband of her panties and tugged them down. She drove her fingers into his hair and lifted her hips as he lowered his head and inhaled the good, clean scent of her.

He parted her with his fingers, then tasted her. She shivered, her thighs tightening against his shoulders. He explored her soft folds, teasing, flicking, stroking until she was panting and arching her back, on the verge of climax. He shed his T-shirt and shorts in record time and surged into her.

He closed his eyes, deliberately fixing this moment, this

sensation in his mind. If he had to have all the bad stuff, all the horror, he should be able to have this, too. And maybe some nights when she was gone he'd dream of her and of being with her instead of the other.

She pulled him down on top of her. They kissed as he stroked in and out of her. He knew she was close and he ran his hands over her breasts and belly and thighs. She called his name, her fingers clenching into his backside. And then she was coming, her head thrown back, her breasts lifting. He drove deep inside her and held her close as his own climax hit him.

He started to roll away from her but she held him still.

"Not yet."

"I'm too heavy."

"No, you're not."

She wrapped her arms around him and he lay on top of her, breathing to her rhythm, feeling her heart beat against his chest. After a while she pressed her face into his neck and inhaled deeply.

"Okay," she sighed.

He smiled faintly as he rolled to one side. "We can do it again if you give me twenty minutes to recover."

"Okay. But the clock is on, Mr. Jones."

She fell asleep after the second time and he lay beside her listening to the sound of her breathing for a long time before he fell asleep.

NATE WOKE IN THE EARLY hours and lay staring at the ceiling in the dark, trying to ignore the promptings of his conscience. After half an hour he eased away from Elizabeth and climbed out of bed. Dressed in only a pair of boxer-briefs, he padded outside to where the recycling bin was stored.

The envelopes were where he'd left them, piled on top of a stack of newspapers. He grabbed them and took them into the kitchen, then he grabbed a knife from the butcher's block and sat at the table.

By the time dawn was turning the sky apricot he'd opened four months' worth of financial reports, marketing strategies and client account summaries. He knew the business was doing okay. Not brilliantly, but okay. Something to be expected in these tough economic times, perhaps, but Smartsell had been on a huge growth curve six months ago and there was still plenty of juice left in the market. Their point of sale and stock keeping program had blown the existing players out of the water when they'd launched four years ago. Their competitors' systems were older, based on inflexible, outdated platforms. Smartsell was cheaper, faster, more efficient and more user-friendly. By rights, the company should still be converting retailers by the bucket load.

Looking over the marketing reports, Nate could see that Jarvie had pulled back on advertising and other promotional activity. Operations and development had always been Nate's responsibility, marketing and roll-out Jarvie's. But it was clear that with Nate's absence from the business, Jarvie was letting marketing flounder in order to keep operations ticking over.

It wasn't a dire picture, by any means. Smartsell was in no danger of folding. But it wasn't the way it should be. Not by a long shot.

He was jotting down notes when the bead curtain rattled and Elizabeth entered the kitchen.

"You're up early," she said. Her gaze took in the discarded envelopes and piles of paper.

"Couldn't sleep."

He sat back and rubbed the heels of his hands against his eyes. Then he looked at her.

"How do you feel about a trip to the city?"

ELIZABETH TRIED TO HIDE her excitement as she drove Nate into Melbourne later that morning. He'd opened the envelopes. He'd absorbed their contents, and now he wanted to reengage with his old life. She was no psychologist, but she figured this had to be a good sign. A great sign. He'd been drinking less lately, too. And although he had never specifically admitted it, she knew he was sleeping better—through the night, in most cases.

Maybe...

Maybe time was working its magic. Maybe his mind was slowly coming to terms with that horrible night and the loss of his sister.

He started giving her directions when they hit one of the main highways into the city, and soon she was pulling up out the front of a high-rise building on a wide, tree-lined boulevard that Nate told her was called St. Kilda Road.

She glanced up at the building, assuming it was Smartsell's headquarters. It was pretty damn impressive. Clearly, Nate and his business partner had done well for themselves.

"I'm probably going to be a while. There's good shopping in the city center, and two art galleries," Nate said as he gathered his papers and jacket.

"Don't worry. If there's a shoe shop, I'll be right for hours."

"There are lots of shoe shops."

He already had her phone number and they agreed he'd call her when he was ready to be collected. She put a hand on his arm when he was about to slide out of the car.

"Good luck."

He smiled tightly and exited the car. It was busy, nearly eleven o'clock, and there were lots of cars speeding past and a steady flow of people in and out of the building. She watched Nate glance around, clearly ill at ease. *She* was finding all the rush and noise and urgency a little overwhelming after only a few weeks on the island. She could only imagine what a culture shock it was for him to be in the thick of commerce again.

He glanced back at her and caught her watching. He forced a smile, then he turned and walked into the building. She stared after him, wishing she could go with him. But Nate would hardly want to have her playing shotgun while he reimmersed himself in his business.

She found parking under one of the big buildings in the city center and made her way into a large department store. Christmas decorations hung from the ceilings and display ends. She hadn't given much thought to Christmas—since meeting Nate the world had devolved to just the two of them.

She spent the next hour searching for suitable gifts for her family. She found a pair of leather gloves for her grandfather and a cashmere shawl in her grandmother's favorite periwinkle-blue. She spotted a set of frilly, silly pajamas that absolutely screamed Violet and added them to her haul.

What to buy Nate presented a bigger problem. The one thing she wished for him in all the world—peace of mind—was not hers to give. Everything else seemed incredibly frivolous by comparison. She settled for buying him a new wallet, since she'd noticed the corner was frayed on his, as well as a bottle of the aftershave she knew he liked.

She waited in line to have her presents wrapped, then she waited in line at the post office to put the bulk of them in the mail. With a bit of luck they'd make it home by Christmas.

She'd had enough of fighting her way through crowds of shoppers by then and she took herself on a tour of the city. She had wandered inside the stately Parliament House and was admiring the Victorian columns and high-arching ceilings when her eye fell on a sign advertising the government departments housed in the building. She paused as she saw that the Department of Education was located on the next level.

Twenty minutes later, she was reading over the sheaf of papers she'd been handed when she asked about applying to work as a teacher in Australia. It seemed a fairly straightforward process, especially since she could now claim an Australian as her parent. She smiled a little grimly to herself. Perhaps Sam Blackwell might be of some use to her, after all.

She was having a coffee in the State Library when Nate called.

"Hi. Are you ready to go?" she asked. She checked her watch and blinked when she saw that it was a quarter to four.

Which meant Nate had been at Smartsell for nearly five hours. That had to be good news.

She wanted to ask how he was doing, how he was feeling, but she knew better than to come right out with it.

"All done. Want to come pick me up?"

"I'm in the city," she said. "I'm not sure how long it will take me, but I'm leaving now."

She gathered the application forms she'd been going over and stuffed them into her handbag, then she walked to the car. Rush hour was starting and it took her nearly half an hour to make her way back to St. Kilda Road where she'd left Nate.

He was standing at the front, a folder of papers in hand, and he walked to the car and got in the moment she pulled over.

"I'm so sorry. I think maybe I came the worst possible way," she said.

"No worries. I figured it'd be pretty busy out there. How was the shopping?"

"Competitive. I nearly had to wrestle a woman to the ground over a cashmere shawl for my grandmother."

He seemed more relaxed than when they'd arrived and

she wondered if she should even raise the thought that had occurred to her on the drive over: the fact that with traffic the way it was, there was no way they'd be able to reach the island before nightfall.

"Nate, it's pretty late. If we head off now…"

His face tightened. "Yeah."

She waited in silence as he mulled the situation over.

"How do you feel about a night in town?" he finally asked.

He didn't look at her. He was embarrassed. Probably ashamed, too, knowing Nate. It wasn't enough that he had to deal with the repercussions of the accident, he had to give himself a hard time for being human, too.

"Great. Then we can drive back first thing in the morning," she said.

"We could do a hotel, or we can go to my place. Your choice."

Nate's place. Useless to pretend she didn't want to see where he lived. But she couldn't help but notice the flat tone in his voice, and the fact that he'd given her a choice.

"Which would you prefer?" she asked.

"I'm not a child, Lizzy. Pick whatever suits you. I don't need to be coddled every step of the goddamned way."

She flinched at the sharp tone in his voice. There was a taut moment of silence in the car, then he sighed heavily.

"Sorry."

He didn't say anything else but he reached across the console and took her hand. She looked at their joined hands, his skin still so much browner than hers.

"I picked up some forms from the education department today," she said in a rush. "The woman at the desk said I'd have no problem having my qualification recognized and registering for work if I wanted to teach in Australia."

She glanced across at him, trying to read his reaction. He was very still, his face expressionless.

"What about your grandparents? Your life back in London?"

"I'll miss them, of course. But London doesn't have you, Nate."

She held her breath, waiting for his response. It wasn't long in coming.

"Bloody hell, Lizzy," he said.

Suddenly she was in his arms, being held so tightly she could hardly breathe.

A slow smile crept across her face.

He wanted her to stay. He was glad she wasn't going home.

"I guess that answers my question, then," she said.

Nate's grip eased and he pulled back so he could look into her face. He lifted a hand and touched the angle of her jaw, then he smoothed a finger along one of her eyebrows.

"Lizzy."

He kissed her, an almost violent, needy, urgent kiss that left her gasping when he finally broke away.

"Hotel or my place?" he asked as they grudgingly let each other go.

She glanced at the hard ridge in his jeans. "Which is closer?"

"My place."

She started the car and looked at him expectantly.

"Take the first left," he said.

She didn't need to be told twice.

11

IT TOOK TEN MINUTES for Elizabeth to drive to Nate's Albert Park home. It had been four months since Nate had been back. It had been too hard, waking up in a space that held so many memories of Olivia.

But if he hadn't wanted to come here, he shouldn't have given Elizabeth a choice.

"Oh, this is like London, with all the grand, la-di-da houses facing the central garden square," Elizabeth said as she pulled up to the front of his house in St. Vincent Place.

"Mmm. Except our garden is public, not private," he said.

"You colonials. I don't know where you get your egalitarian values from."

She gave him a cheeky look as she got out of the car. When he joined her on the pavement she was staring up at his house.

"Very elegant," she said with an approving nod. "Did you choose the colors?"

He shook his head and knew she'd guessed that Olivia had.

"Well, she had excellent taste. I love the taupe facade with the glossy black lacework."

Nate concentrated on finding the right key on his key ring. "She was great at all that sort of stuff. Designing clothes, colors, music. She was always working on something."

Because he couldn't delay it any longer, he opened the front gate and walked up the short path to the elaborately tiled porch.

His key slid into the lock and the door opened. He inhaled the smell of beeswax and sunshine and the faintest, lightest hint of raspberry lip gloss. Olivia's favorite.

Elizabeth followed him inside, her footsteps echoing loudly on the wooden floor.

"This is lovely, too. Are you going to give me a tour?" she asked, glancing up the wide hallway.

There was no expectation in her tone. She was simply asking, giving him the opportunity to say yes or no as suited him. As usual, her cool, matter-of-fact approach gave him the breathing room he needed to adjust.

"It's not exactly a mansion, but I'll do my best to get us lost," he said.

He led her through the airy, light living room and listened as she admired the cream-and-taupe decor, then through to the country-style kitchen with its white cabinets and pine counters and old-fashioned butler's sink. She ran a hand over the smooth, worn surface of his French provincial dining table, one of Olivia's must-haves from a local antique dealer, then walked through to the more casual and modern family room with its modular furniture and huge flat-screen TV.

"Your sister had a good eye," she said. She wandered over to the French doors and looked out at the garden.

He moved to stand beside her. He'd paid the cleaner to come in once a week and air the place out, but the garden had been let go and the flower beds were bristling with weeds. The splash of bright red at the end of the garden drew his eye to the cheerful smiling grill of Olivia's Mini Cooper parked to one side of the double car port. He'd bought it for her for her seventeenth birthday so she could learn to drive. She'd never had a chance to take it out on her own.

He turned away in time to see Elizabeth pick up a photo frame from the bookshelf. He and Olivia at the beach. She was only fourteen and just showing the promise of the beauty she would one day become.

Elizabeth studied the photograph for a long moment, then she returned it to the bookshelf without saying anything and he led her into the hall and up the stairs.

"Spare bedroom, bathroom, study, my room," he said, pointing to each doorway as they walked past. He didn't mention the closed door at the other end of the hall.

Elizabeth stepped into his room and assessed the king-size bed and black-and-white photography on his walls with one sweeping glance. Then she reached for the buttons on her shirt and started to undress.

"Correct me if I'm wrong, but I believe there was an implied promise of sex upon arrival," she said when he simply stood and watched her.

She let her shirt fall down her arms and crossed the room to slide her arms around him. She hugged him tightly for a long beat, then she began undoing his belt and unzipping his jeans.

Despite the weight bearing down on him, he felt himself becoming aroused. He took charge, walking her back toward his bed and pushing her down onto the mattress.

She watched as he stepped out of his jeans. He pushed up her skirt and pulled her panties down, then he slid his fingers into her slick folds and teased her, watching her face all the while. Her eyes grew heavy-lidded and she bit her lip. Her muscles tightened around him when he slid a finger inside her. He kept it there as he used his thumb to stroke her. She lifted her hips and clenched her hands in the quilt cover and moaned low in her throat.

He knew her sounds by now and he gripped his cock in his hand and stroked the slick seam of her sex with it, up and down, up and down.

"Yes, Nate, please," she pleaded.

He slid inside her in small degrees, reveling in the way she sighed when he finally filled her.

Then there was just the slide of skin on skin and her hands gripping his shoulders and arms and backside as he pumped into her. They came together, shuddering out their pleasure in counterpoint. He rested his forehead on the bed beside her for a long moment afterward, then he turned his head and kissed her.

"Thank you," he said quietly.

She didn't say a word, but he knew she understood. She always did.

They ordered in for dinner—Thai takeout from the place around the corner. Elizabeth insisted on them sharing a bath afterward and her skin was still damp when they made love for the second time later that night.

She fell asleep afterward. Nate waited until she was breathing deeply before climbing out of bed and walking barefoot to Olivia's room.

The doorknob was cool in his hand and he hesitated a moment. Did he really want to do this? He closed his eyes for a long beat. Then he twisted the doorknob and pushed the door open. He flicked the light on and blinked in the sudden bright.

Everything was as she'd left it. If he didn't know any better, he'd think his sister had simply stepped out for the night. Her iPod lay abandoned on her bedside table, the wires for her earphones dangling to the floor. A pair of jeans were thrown over the end of the bed and her usual clutter covered her dressing table—makeup and books and notes to herself and jewelry. He fingered one of her rings, picked up a book and opened it to where she'd bent the page to mark her spot.

He returned to the bed and sat on it. He knew he should pack up her room, that it was morbid and maybe even unhealthy to leave it this way, but there was so much of her in here: the photos she'd taped to the walls, the quilt she'd made for the bed and the curtains for the window. He didn't want to pack it away. He wasn't ready to say goodbye yet.

Grief closed his throat and he reached for her iPod to distract himself. The battery was dead, so he opened the bedside drawer instead. Her diary was in there, along with a jumble of pens and the old slide phone she'd abandoned when the iPhone became the must-have accessory of the year. The dull shine of light on foil caught his eye and he shifted her diary to one side and picked up the small, square packet.

A condom.

He ran his thumb over the giveaway circle beneath the foil. Six months ago he would have been unthrilled in the extreme to find this in his sister's drawer. Like any big brother, he'd hated the idea of her being hurt or taken advantage of or vulnerable.

Now, he hoped like hell that she'd had the pleasure of being skin to skin with someone she cared about before she died. He hoped she'd experienced lust and joy and desire.

He hoped—

He closed his hand, crushing the foil packet within his fist. For a long moment he sat, his head bowed. Then he stood and flicked off the light and went back to bed.

NATE WAS QUIET IN THE morning and Elizabeth did her best to lighten his mood. She insisted that he take her to his favorite local breakfast place, then she suggested a walk through the nearby market. By the time they returned to the house and

Nate had grabbed some extra clothes from his wardrobe it was midafternoon and he was smiling more readily.

She couldn't help wondering if that was because she'd done such a great job distracting him or because they were leaving this beautiful, sad house and its ghosts behind.

She kept up a steady stream of chatter as she drove to the island, telling him what she'd bought for her grandparents for Christmas and challenging him to guess what she'd bought for him. She'd been hoping he might reciprocate by talking about his experience at Smartsell the previous day but he didn't and she reminded herself that Nate had been living in his self-created, hermetically sealed isolation for a long time. When he was ready to share, he would.

They drove over the San Remo bridge just after five. They stopped in town to get groceries, and it was nearly six by the time she turned into their street. A shiny black sports car was parked in the driveway at Nate's place and she slowed as she approached the house.

"That's Jarvie's car, isn't it?" she asked, recognizing it from Jarvie's last visit.

"Yeah."

The driver's door on the sports car opened as she parked at the curb, and Nate's business partner stood, pulling off his sunglasses and tossing them into the car. He stared through the windshield at Nate, his expression grim.

"What's going on, Nate?" she asked, but he was already opening his door and getting out.

She didn't understand why Jarvie was here and why he was looking so thunderous. He and Nate had spent almost the whole day together yesterday, and even though Nate hadn't spoken about it last night, he'd seemed happy enough with his day's work. So why was Jarvie looking as if he wanted to rip the head off something?

She scrambled to exit the car and was in time to see Jarvie

toss a folder at Nate. Nate was too slow to catch it and the folder hit his chest and bounced off, sending a sheaf of closely typed pages fanning across the front lawn.

"No. Never gonna happen. You got that?" Jarvie said.

Nate shrugged. "If you don't want it, I'll offer it to someone else."

"You can't do that," Jarvie said.

"According to my lawyer, I can. If I offer my half of the business to you and you don't want it, I'm free to sell it to someone who is mutually acceptable to both of us."

Elizabeth stood to one side, trying to catch up with what was going on. Nate was selling his half of the business? And why was he talking about his lawyers?

"No one is going to be acceptable to me. We started that business together, Nate. You and me."

"If you look over the offer, it's more than fair. I know you can raise the funds. In a couple of years, you'll be debt free and Smartsell will be all yours."

Nate's voice and demeanor were very calm and reasonable and she realized that he'd been expecting this. Which was why he hadn't seemed surprised to see Jarvie waiting for them when they pulled up.

"You didn't go to Smartsell yesterday," she guessed. "You went to your lawyer, didn't you?"

Nate glanced at her. She saw the answer in his eyes.

"What's wrong with the way things have been going?" Jarvie said. "I know I've been bugging you, and I'll back off if that's what you want. But selling out is a mistake, Nate. When you've had some more time, when you're ready to come back into the business—"

"That's never going to happen."

"Bullshit. I know the accident knocked you around. You're cut up about Olivia. But you'll get past it and you'll want back in and I'm more than happy to wait—"

"You need to listen to what I'm saying, okay? It's over. Smartsell isn't fine, it needs more focus. You need to move on, and I'm holding you back. Take the offer, Jarvie."

"No."

"Then I'll sell to someone else."

Jarvie's jaw bunched. He took a step toward Nate. Elizabeth tensed, worried things were going to get physical. Jarvie was so wound up and Nate so determined....

"Don't do this. You don't need to. Smartsell will wait. We'll wait as long as it takes."

"Trust me. In a few days' time, you'll realize this is the best option for everyone."

Nate turned to go but Jarvie grabbed the front of his shirt in both fists.

"You can't just walk away. Not this time. I won't let you. This was our dream, man. We freaking well clawed that business up out of nothing. You can't flush all that away." Jarvie's face was stark with anger and grief. "I don't want to do this without you, man," he said, his voice catching. "Please, think about what you're doing."

Elizabeth pressed her fingertips against her lips. The emotion on Jarvie's face was so raw, so intimate, she had to look away.

"Let me go," Nate said. He tried to pull free but Jarvie wouldn't release him.

"You can't throw everything away because of one bad thing, Nate. You've got a life, a good life. You can't trash it. You can't walk away from everything, change everything..."

Jarvie's voice broke and he lowered his head, his knuckles showing white as he clasped Nate's shirt. Nate didn't say anything, simply waited patiently as he stared over Jarvie's shoulder.

The expression on his face made Elizabeth's blood run cold. She'd thought he was getting better, slowly but surely.

She'd thought yesterday had been a huge step forward. But the bleakness she saw, the resignation…

After a long, tense moment, Jarvie unclenched his hands. Nate hovered for a beat as though some other force held him, then he turned and strode into the street and took the track to the beach.

12

ELIZABETH GLANCED AT JARVIE. The other man's face was twisted with grief and she immediately looked away again. She bent and began collecting the papers strewn across the lawn to give him a moment to compose himself. After a short beat, Jarvie joined her. They worked in silence, then she stood and handed her stack of papers over to him.

"Would you like to come in for a cup of coffee?"

He shook his head. "I need to get back. But thanks."

He walked to his car. She wanted to say more to him, to reassure him that Nate would change his mind, that this decision to opt out of the business once and for all was only a knee-jerk reaction. But she knew it hadn't been. Nate had stayed up half the night reviewing the accumulated Smartsell paperwork. Then he'd made a very cold, very considered decision and asked her to drive him to the city so he could act on it.

Jarvie's engine fired and she stepped to one side as the car shot out into the street. Gravel spurted under the wide tires as the car took off.

She walked up the driveway, and with each step her anger grew. Nate had made huge decisions—major, life-changing decisions—and hadn't said a word to her during the two-hour

drive to the city. He hadn't said a word last night, either, or
this afternoon when they drove home again. She'd told him
about her plans to apply for a teaching job in Melbourne—to
move *countries,* goddamn it—and he'd been sitting on this
huge, monumental decision all along.

She unlocked the house, then stood in the kitchen frowning
and fuming and feeling helpless. Nate selling his half of the
business was a mistake—a huge one. The life he was living
now—this small niche he'd carved out for himself of sun and
surf and sex and beer—was a coping mechanism, a holding
pattern. It wasn't forever. It certainly wasn't the measure of
his world. She understood that perhaps he couldn't see that
right now, that he was too busy surviving one day at a time
and keeping his demons at bay, but she could and she knew
that he would regret divesting himself of what was once obviously a huge part of his life.

So many times over the past few weeks she'd bitten her
tongue and chosen not to push Nate. But maybe she should
have. Maybe she should have urged him to find a therapist, or
return to his therapist, if he'd ever had one. She'd been quietly
encouraging him to drink less and open up more, but maybe
she should have forced him to talk every time he clammed up
instead of waiting for him to talk in his own stubborn time.

She sighed and pushed her fingers through her hair. She
didn't know. She wasn't an expert. She'd simply been following her instincts where he was concerned, but maybe they'd
been wrong.

She looked at the clock on the kitchen wall. He'd been
gone for nearly half an hour. If he was acting true to form, he
wouldn't be back for hours yet.

It was nearly full dark by now. She paced a little, then
decided to have a quick shower to wash away the stress of the
past few hours. Maybe by the time she was done Nate would

be back and they could have the heart-to-heart they so sorely needed.

She headed into the bathroom and turned the shower on. Water sprayed out onto the bathroom floor and she tugged the shower door closed to stop the tiles from getting soaked while she undressed. The door slid two inches before jumping its tracks and wedging itself open. She ground her teeth. This was exactly what she didn't need. She gave the screen an experimental tug, but it didn't budge.

Is it too much to ask for this one thing to go right? This one little thing?

Setting her jaw, she got a grip on the jammed panel and tried to force it into moving. For some reason it seemed incredibly important that she solve this problem right now.

"Stupid blooming thing."

She and the door remained locked in mortal combat for a full twenty seconds as she grunted and pushed and pulled. She was about to give up when the door suddenly gave with a clattering rush. She staggered, off balance, and her feet slipped on the wet tiles.

Instinctively she flailed to try and regain her balance. Her hand smashed into the glass of the shower door and it splintered with an almighty crack. She felt a lancing pain as jagged glass slashed into her arm. She barely had time to register the sting before blood spurted from the wound.

It was so red and there seemed to be so much of it so quickly that for a moment she simply stood there, transfixed. There was blood dripping down her arm, blood on the glass, blood circling the shower drain, blood on the bathroom floor.

In the back of her mind, a calm voice told her that she needed to stop the flow—quickly. The towel was on the floor and she squatted to pick it up. The world went black around the edges at the movement and she dropped to her knees.

She blinked, fighting the dizziness. The last thing she

wanted to do right now was faint. Not while her arm was bleeding freely.

Warmth dripped from her fingers in an unending stream and she folded the towel with her left hand and wrapped it around her right forearm. She glanced down at the wound as she did so and immediately wished she hadn't. A long, gaping slit bisected her forearm and she could see the deep red of muscle.

The dizziness hit again and she pressed the towel tightly over the gash. She remembered that she'd read somewhere that she should raise it, too, to keep the wound above her heart. Or was that for a snake bite? She shook her head. It was hard to think straight.

Belatedly it occurred to her that she needed an ambulance.

Talk about being slow off the mark—an ambulance should have been the first thing she'd thought of. Her right arm pressed to her side and her left hand clamped over the towel, she leaned her shoulder against the bathroom wall and tried to stand so she could reach the phone in the kitchen. Her thighs quivered with the effort and her vision got dark around the edges again. She sank back onto the floor.

Fine. She'd crawl to the phone. Not a problem.

But even that was beyond her trembling limbs. She looked down and saw that the towel was soaked through and it occurred to her that she was in big trouble. Really big.

She closed her eyes, and all she could think of was Nate. If she didn't get to a phone, she'd never see him again. The past few weeks would be it. Short and sweet. She would never see him recover. She would never get a chance to tell him that she loved him. He would come home and find her and the blood... God, no, she couldn't do that to him. She had to move. Had to.

Somehow she rolled onto her knees. Her shoulder against

the wall, she made it to the hallway. She stared at the distant rectangle of the kitchen doorway. It seemed a very long way away. But she had to keep moving.

Move or die, Lizzy.

The voice in her head spoke with Nate's voice, in the exact tone he used when he was ordering her about on the *Ducky*. She tucked her head into her chest and shuffled forward another foot.

Come on, Lizzy. Pick it up. Snoozers are losers.

She grit her teeth and fought against the horrible weakness stealing over her. It was only fifteen feet away. She could crawl fifteen feet. Of course she could.

NATE SAT ON THE BEACH until it was almost full dark. He thought about going to the pub, but he knew Elizabeth was waiting for him at home. With questions, no doubt.

He'd done the right thing. For Smartsell, for Jarvie. For himself. He had. Absolutely.

And yet doubt still gnawed at him. He and Jarvie had spent countless hours sweating in his rental apartment while they perfected the code for Smartsell 1.0. They'd recruited a handful of retailers and offered the prototype software for free, then they'd risked everything they owned to get a business loan to finance their start-up. Nathan had been so determined to make it work. His mother had been sick by then and he'd known it would soon be just him and Olivia. He'd been terrified of letting her down, not providing for her, not giving her everything she would have had if their parents were alive. He'd worked around the clock, tirelessly. He'd given the business his blood, sweat and tears and he'd loved every minute of it. Been fiercely proud and more than a little bit cocky. For a while he'd even gone a little overboard—the expensive car, the big house, lots of splashy dinners. Then he and Jarvie had settled into their success and starting really digging in and building the business.

And then he'd had the accident, and the world had shifted on its axis and all the rules had changed.

Olivia was gone. All that effort, and she was gone and none of it meant a thing. The money, the house, the success—he'd swap it all in a heartbeat to have her back. But that was never going to happen.

The tide was starting to come in. He watched the waves chase each other up the sand for a few more minutes, then pushed himself to his feet. Shoes in hand, he trudged up the beach.

The kitchen light was on as he walked up the driveway. He tossed his shoes beside the back steps and entered the house.

He'd expected to find Elizabeth making dinner, but the kitchen was empty. He was about to go check the studio to see if she was out there when something caught the corner of his eye. He glanced toward the hallway and saw a figure huddled on the carpet. Dread thumped low in his belly and he lunged forward.

She was unconscious, her face gray, and there was blood everywhere—on her chest, down her jeans, smeared along the carpet. A towel was wrapped around her forearm, the fabric stained crimson.

"Lizzy. Jesus."

He threw himself to his knees and pressed his trembling fingers to her neck. A pulse throbbed faintly against his fingers. He let his breath out on a relieved hiss.

She was alive. Thank God.

He and Jarvie had insisted all their staff have first-aid training, and snatches of information flashed across his mind. He needed to stop the bleeding by binding it and elevating her arm. Then he needed to get her to help because she'd lost a lot of blood.

Memories from another night threatened to take over but he pushed them away and scrambled to his feet again. He flung open the hall cupboard, snatching up a handful of clean towels. Then he was at her side again, pulling the soaked towel off her arm. His stomach lurched when he saw the extent of her injury. Quickly he wrapped the towel around her arm, pulling it brutally tight. He held it in place while he dragged his belt off one-handed and used the leather strap to cinch the towel in place. Then he lifted Elizabeth's hand and held it upright while he dragged his cell phone from his back pocket.

He was starting to shake and his hands were so slick with her blood he fumbled the number for emergency services. He tried again, his gaze constantly flicking to Elizabeth's face. She was so pale. So goddamned pale. And her hand in his was so cold....

"Emergency services. Please state the nature of the emergency."

"I need an ambulance. She's cut herself, I don't know how. There's a lot of blood. She's unconscious."

"Sir, you're calling from a cell and I can't pinpoint your location. Do you have an address for me?"

"It's 14 Radcliffe Street, Cowes."

"Cowes on Phillip Island?"

"That's right. How soon can you get an ambulance here? She's lost a lot of blood."

"Is it a private residence, sir?"

"Yes. Tell me how long it's going to take?" He was yelling, but he didn't give a shit. Elizabeth needed help now.

"Sir, I'm checking the system and there has been a car accident near the bridge and all three ambulances on the island are in attendance. The wait time is thirty minutes."

"What? No!"

"Sir. I need you to remain calm. Are you able to get the victim to hospital yourself? The nearest emergency facility is Wonthaggi Hospital. I can give you directions."

Nate closed his eyes for a brief second.

"I know where it is."

Wonthaggi Hospital was where they'd taken him after the accident.

"Tell them I'm coming in," he said.

He ended the call and shoved the phone into his pocket. Then he slid his arms beneath Elizabeth and lifted her. He surged to his feet and headed for the door, not thinking about what he'd committed to doing.

She'd left the car keys on the kitchen counter and he leaned to one side to snatch them up. Then he was racing down the back steps and down the driveway to the car. Somehow he got the car door open, then he slid her into the front passenger seat, cranking it back as far as it would go before clicking her seat belt on. He slammed the door shut and ran around to the driver's side.

His subconscious was way ahead of him as he slid into the driver's seat. His whole body was already trembling, his breathing was shallow, his chest tight. Nausea burned the back of his throat as he pulled the driver's door shut and shoved the key into the ignition.

Don't think about it, just do it. Just do it.

His teeth started chattering as he slammed the car into reverse and planted his foot. The car swerved out into the street.

The feel of the wheel beneath his hand, the closeness of the roof, the dark pressing in from outside...

He pushed the car into Drive and took off, panting and shaking.

Don't think about it, don't think about it.

Olivia's screams filled his ears, begging him to help her.

He was clammy with sweat and his breathing was so loud he could hear himself gasping.

There was no traffic and he sped toward the intersection with Main Street. He signaled, checked the road and turned. Headlights flashed across the interior of the car and he swerved instinctively toward the curb. The other car drove past and he realized it was on the opposite side of the road and there had never been any danger of the two cars crossing paths.

I can't do this. I can't do this. I can't do this.

The knowledge gripped him with dread certainty. He couldn't make himself put his foot down. He was paralyzed, utterly powerless against the adrenaline and remembered trauma storming his mind. He closed his eyes and leaned forward, pressing his forehead into the hard plastic of the steering wheel.

She's going to die, you bastard. Lizzy is going to die if you don't get your freaking act together and drive.

He bared his teeth in an anguished grimace and banged his head once, twice, three times against the steering wheel. The small, sharp pain served to focus him, dragging him back from the edge.

Breathe. Breathe, you bastard. Put your foot down and save her.

He sucked in big belly breaths. Then he sat back in the driver's seat and checked the road and pulled away from the curb.

The car surged into the night. He kept breathing into his solar plexus. Fighting the fear with every muscle in his body. His hands gripped the wheel so tightly his knuckles ached.

Slowly the initial panic receded, leaving him shaky and so freaking grateful he'd survived that tears pricked his eyes.

"It's going to be okay, Lizzy. We're going to get through this," he said.

She didn't respond and he glanced at her. She was very still.

He released his death grip on the wheel to press his fingers into her neck again. Her pulse fluttered against his fingers, faint but detectable.

She was alive. She had a chance. Renewed determination flooded through him. He flattened his foot to the floor and watched as the speedometer rose past a hundred.

Time seemed to ebb and flow in strange, unpredictable surges as he sped through the night. Trees flashed by outside, but it took forever to reach the San Remo bridge, and then suddenly the signs for Dalyston were flashing by and he knew he only had about eight kilometers to go until he hit the outskirts of Wonthaggi.

He pulled his phone from his pocket and called to the hospital, letting them know he was minutes away.

A low moan tore his attention from the road as he passed the first outlying houses of Wonthaggi township, and he glanced over to see Elizabeth's eyes flickering open.

"Lizzy. It's all right. We're almost at the hospital. Stay still, sweetheart. We're nearly there."

He touched her shoulder reassuringly. Jesus, she was so cold and clammy.

"Nate." Her voice was barely a whisper.

"I'm here, sweetheart. We're all good."

She frowned as her wavering gaze focused on him. "You're driving."

"Hang in there, Lizzy."

She lifted her good hand and made a feeble attempt to touch him.

"So proud of you," she said weakly.

Her eyes fluttered closed again.

Nate took the final turn at full speed. The hospital's blue-and-white sign was a beacon at the end of the street. He slewed into the emergency drive and slammed his fist onto the horn as he braked sharply. Then he was out of the car and running around to the passenger door as the medical staff barreled outside with a stretcher.

"We'll take her, sir," a nurse said, pulling him out of the way.

"Do you know what blood type she is?" someone else demanded.

"No. But she's lost a lot. I tried to keep her arm elevated…"

The team transferred Elizabeth to the stretcher with practiced efficiency. Then she was being rushed through the double doors, the attending doctor yelling instructions.

Nate was left behind, hands hanging slack by his sides.

He'd made it.

He'd been convinced that he would never drive again, but he'd conquered his fear and he'd made it. He'd gotten Lizzy the help she needed.

When push had come to shove, he'd battled his demons and won.

He didn't feel a rush of triumph, however.

He didn't feel anything.

ELIZABETH WOKE TO THE SMELL of antiseptic and the sound of voices. She frowned and tried to roll onto her side but something was holding her back. She protested groggily and forced her eyes open, only to blink in surprise when she registered the overwhelming white of a hospital room.

What on earth…?

Then it all came rushing back—the trip to Melbourne, Jarvie and Nate's confrontation, the shower door, trying to get to the phone.

Nate driving her to the hospital.

She frowned. Was she remembering correctly? But the

picture in her head was indelible—Nate behind the wheel, telling her not to move, telling her everything was going to be all right.

She lifted her head, but the chair by her bed was empty.

Where was he? She was so proud of him. He'd driven her to safety. He'd saved her life. She wanted to see him and talk to him and thank him and tell him all the things she'd kept inside.

She reached for the buzzer pinned to her pillowcase, automatically using her right hand. Pain washed up her arm and she subsided with a groan.

She was so incredibly tired. Utterly washed out. She let her head drop on the pillow and realized there was an IV drip beside the bed, the tube attached to her other arm.

Weariness made her eyelids heavy. She let them fall closed. She'd rest for a minute, then she'd call someone and ask all the questions teeming in her mind.…

When she woke again the hospital was quieter, the lights dimmer. Nighttime, then. But which nighttime? How many days had passed? She twisted her head to see if Nate was there but again the chair beside her bed was empty. She subsided onto her pillow. Where was he? She wanted to see him. She *needed* to see him.

She sniffed, aware that she was feeling very sorry for herself and not a little weepy. Then movement at the door caught her eye and she turned her head in time to catch a figure retreating away from the doorway.

"Nate?" she called.

No one answered.

"Nate? Is that you?"

Still no response. She shifted higher on her pillows, which was when it occurred to her that the figure had been too short to be Nate. He was much bigger and broader.

So where was he?

A young dark-haired nurse entered the room, a tray in hand. "You're awake. Excellent. I'm Jodie, I'll be looking after you tonight. How are you feeling? How's your pain level?"

She slid the tray onto the table at the foot of Elizabeth's bed.

"Um. I'm fine. A little uncomfortable but not overly so. Can you tell me, there was a man in the doorway just now...?"

Jodie shook her head. "Sorry. I didn't see anyone. Might have been one of the other patients' visitors. Although it's well past visiting hours. Do you feel up to eating?"

"I don't know."

"Maybe some soup and some juice? You've lost a lot of blood and even though you've had a transfusion food will definitely help to get you back on track."

"All right. I'll try some soup," Elizabeth said.

Jodie helped her sit up, propping an extra pillow behind her.

"Can I ask—has anyone been in to see me? A tall, dark man? Blue eyes?" *Really sexy, utterly gorgeous? Love of my life?*

"I'm sorry, no. Not that I know of. I can check at the nurses' station to see if there are any messages for you, though?"

"Thanks."

Jodie moved the table closer and removed the plastic cover from the bowl of soup on the tray.

"Chicken vegetable, and for a change it's actually quite edible," she said with a wry wink.

Elizabeth tried to smile but all she could manage was a weak twist of her lips. She didn't understand. Nathan had driven her to the hospital. Why wasn't he here?

She ate the soup and half a bowl of yogurt, then she had a visit from her doctor who explained that she'd cut her radial artery and that despite having received a blood transfusion she'd need to take it very easy while her body recovered.

"The stitches can come out in seven to ten days, and the nutritionist will be around to talk to you about your diet. You'll need to take in a lot of protein for the next six to eight weeks."

"When can I go home?" she asked.

"We need to do a few tests tomorrow, but there's no reason why you can't leave afterward as long as you're prepared to take it very easy. Lots of bed rest, no standing quickly, no heavy lifting."

She nodded dutifully and waited patiently while the doctor conferred with her nurse at the foot of her bed. Then they left and she was alone again. She sighed and rolled onto her left side, facing the window. She felt incredibly alone and the sudden, childish urge to call her grandparents overtook her. Just to hear the sound of their voices. She couldn't, of course. Not from hospital. No way would her grandmother's health cope with learning Elizabeth had had an accident on the other side of the world. And her grandfather would insist on flying out to see her, and he'd want her to come straight home the moment she was good to fly....

She could call Violet, however. She was reaching for the phone when she glanced up and saw a reflection in the window—a man hovering in her doorway, a pair of crutches propped beneath his armpits.

She shuffled around in bed but by the time she'd gotten herself turned around Sam Blackwell was gone.

"I know you're there, Sam," she called.

There was a brief silence, then Sam returned to the doorway. There was no mistaking the chagrin on his face—he looked like a kid caught with his hand in the cookie jar.

Despite everything—his dismissive attitude, his abrupt departure—her heart squeezed at the sight of him.

Stupid heart. She reminded herself that this man had already disappointed her more than once.

"Why are you here?" she asked coolly.

"Nate called me." He remained in the doorway, unprepared to make even the small commitment of entering her room.

"I see. And you rushed straight to my bedside, I take it?"

She was being sarcastic, but the fiery blush that swept up his neck and into his cheeks gave her pause.

Had he really come rushing to her side, then? Was that what that fierce blush was about?

"Why? Why bother when you didn't even want to give me the time of day back on the island?"

His gaze slid over her shoulder to focus on the water jug on her bedside table. "Wanted to make sure you were all right."

She pushed herself higher in the bed and eyed him across several feet of scuffed linoleum.

"If we're going to have this conversation, could you at least come into the room so I don't have to shout? I assume there might be some patients next door who'd like to get some sleep."

He entered the room with visible reluctance. If it wasn't so heartbreaking, it might almost be funny.

"I thought you weren't interested in me?" she asked.

"I never said that. Don't put words in my mouth."

"Well, someone has to, since you never say anything for yourself."

Bugger being polite. She'd tiptoed around him enough.

"I was doing what I thought was best. That's all you need to know."

Elizabeth slapped her good hand palm-down onto the bed. "No, damn you, that's not all I need to know! I'm your daughter, Sam. The very least you can do is look me in the eye and tell me why you don't want anything to do with me. I've had a bloody gutful of people deciding what's best for me—my grandparents, my fiancé. I'm the one who gets to decide what's best for me, not you."

Sam frowned. "Fiancé? I thought you and Nate were on with each other? Don't tell me he's proposed?"

Elizabeth shook her head. "No. I'm not telling you a thing until you explain why you left and why you're here now and why it's *for the best* that you ignore me."

She eyed him belligerently. She wasn't going to give an inch until he offered her something. Some sign that he cared.

He stared at the ground, his hands opening and closing on the hand rests of his crutches. The fierce frown on his forehead told her he was debating something internally. She held her breath, waiting. If he turned away now, she knew in her heart that she would never see him again. It would be over, for good.

His chin came up and at last he met her eyes.

"All right. You want to know, I'll tell you. Then you can tell me to go to hell and we'll be right back where we started from."

She didn't say anything, simply waited.

"I met your mother in Greece. She'd just finished school and was traveling with friends. She was good fun, beautiful, loved a party. We, um, hit it off right away. Then her friends went home and Elle decided to stay on, and even though I had a charter I was supposed to crew on, I stayed on, too, and we got a little place on one of the islands, down near the water."

Elizabeth frowned. It was strange to hear her mother's name shortened and to hear that the cool, slightly sad woman she'd known as her mother had once been a party girl, someone a young man could "hit it off" with.

"Did you love her?"

Her father shrugged, not meeting her eyes. "We were both nineteen years old. What did we know?"

Elizabeth decided to count that as a yes.

"She told me she was pregnant after the first month. I—" Sam brushed a hand over his face, momentarily hiding his expression from her. After a minute he started talking again. "I didn't take it well. I was angry. She was supposed to be on the pill. I thought she was trying to trap me. I took off. Took a charter to Turkey. Left her all on her own, with nothing."

Elizabeth frowned. "What does that mean, with nothing?"

"What does it sound like?" Sam said, his tone sharp. "No money, no food, no way of getting home or getting help. She was in trouble with her parents for staying on, so she couldn't turn to them. Her friends had gone. But I didn't think about any of that. I wanted to take off, so I did."

Elizabeth could hear the self-condemnation in his tone. She spared a thought for her nineteen-year-old mother, pregnant and abandoned by her lover in a foreign country.

"What happened then? I take it she went home to England?"

"I don't know. I wasn't around, was I? I always assumed she called your grandparents."

Elizabeth looked at her hands. It wasn't exactly a beautiful romance, but there was nothing particularly surprising in it, either. Her father had behaved like a selfish, immature young man, and her mother had paid the price for her youthful impulsiveness. It was a story as old as time.

"After a while, I got to thinking. I'd had a few good charters, I was offered a steward's job, regular work. I started thinking that maybe having a kid wouldn't be so bad, that I'd be able to look after the two of you without things changing that much. So I hitched a ride to England with a mate and went to find Elle.

"She'd had you by then. I tracked her down, went around to see her at your grandparents' place. They didn't want me to talk to her, but she said she wanted to see me. She brought you downstairs with her. You were—"

Sam cleared his throat.

"You were really small. Lots of blond hair. Big blue eyes, like my mom's. Elle told me that she'd met a new bloke, that they were getting married. That the new guy wanted to adopt you. Then he came in and I realized I'd left my run too late. I'd stuffed up and I'd missed out."

Sam lowered his head and wiped his mouth with the back of his hand.

She waited for him to say more, but he didn't.

She frowned. She didn't understand. If that was the extent of the story, what possible reason could he have had to keep her at arm's length? From what he was saying, he'd come looking for her. A little late in the day, perhaps, but he had still wanted to claim her. And yet he was standing here, unable to look her in the eye.

"There's something else, isn't there?" she guessed.

He glanced toward the door, his reluctance palpable. Then he sighed and lifted his head.

"I could dress it up, tell you how your new dad sweet-talked me and your grandfather leaned on me. But it doesn't change what happened. After Elle took you upstairs to put you down for your afternoon nap, your grandfather came in with his checkbook."

Elizabeth stared at him. "They offered you money to stay away from me?"

"And I took it." He held her eye as he said it, and she could see how deeply the shame ran in him.

"How much?"

"Ten thousand."

"What did you do with it?" Her throat was tight.

"Drank it, mostly. I kept telling myself I was going to put it toward a boat, or put it in a trust and send it to you when you were eighteen or something noble like that. But I drank it, bit by bit. Pissed it up against the wall."

There was a profound silence in the room. Elizabeth could hear the squeak of rubber soles in the corridor outside and the rattle of a curtain being pulled around a bed in the room across the way.

She didn't know what to think. What to say. At the ripe old age of twenty her father had taken ten thousand pounds to disappear from her life and pretend he'd never existed. He'd sold off his claim to her.

"So now you know." Sam's voice was gravelly with suppressed emotion. "You know what kind of man I am, and you know why I figured it was best to make myself scarce."

He turned toward the door. White-hot anger burned inside her as she watched her father prepare to walk away from her for the third time in her life.

"I get it. You don't deserve to know me and so you're taking yourself off. Am I getting this straight?" she said.

He stilled. His face was in profile to her but she knew she'd struck home.

"You're a real saint, aren't you? Sure, you walked away from me once for money, but this time it's because you're protecting me from yourself. How very damned noble of you."

He swung to face her.

"You telling me you want me hanging around? A man who'd sell his own kid?"

"As opposed to what? Having nothing? Knowing there's a man out there in the world who gave me life who I don't know anything about?"

"Some would say that's a better deal."

"Well, they're not me. They didn't grow up in a big house with two old people who didn't know what to do with a little girl who missed her parents so badly she cried herself to sleep every night for six months."

Her voice had risen and a nurse appeared in the doorway to her room.

"Is everything okay in here?"

"Yes," Elizabeth said at the same time that her father did.

They looked at each other. After a moment the nurse shrugged and walked away.

"I want to know where I come from," Elizabeth said. "I want to know my own father."

She could hear the emotion vibrating in her voice and she blinked furiously. Her father stared at her for a long moment. Then he made his way to the chair beside her bed. He slid his crutches from beneath his arms but didn't immediately sit. He looked at her, as though he was waiting for her to object. As though he still couldn't quite believe she was giving him this second chance.

She didn't say anything. He was her father. She wanted a relationship with him, even if he wasn't perfect.

After a few seconds he lowered himself into the chair.

13

THEY TALKED INTO THE small hours, until Elizabeth couldn't keep her eyes open any longer. She learned that her father had had an interesting life, full of adventure. A lonely life, too. He'd never settled down with another woman and she was his only child. Reading between the lines, she guessed that the events of thirty years ago still weighed heavily on him.

He was as interested in her life as she was in his. He listened quietly as she filled in the blanks for him, asking questions, occasionally passing comment. By the time he stood to take up his crutches again she had a solid sense that there was a relationship to be had—if they both wanted it. She hoped that the habit of isolation wasn't so ingrained in her father that he'd revert to his earlier distance. But only time would tell.

She asked about Nate before Sam left. He had no information for her. Nate had called him to let him know what had happened, told Sam where she was, and ended the call without saying anything else.

Despite being bone-weary, Elizabeth lay on her side staring out the darkened window for a long time after her father had gone.

Why hadn't Nate called or come by?

A nervous, fluttery anxiety tightened her belly as she tried to understand. Perhaps he had been unable to find someone to drive him to the hospital. Just because he'd conquered his fears to drive during an emergency did not mean he was cured, after all. Post-traumatic stress was an ongoing condition, not something that was healed with the flick of a switch.

But even if he'd been unable to catch a lift, he could have called. And he hadn't.

Something was wrong, and she was worried.

When she'd woken and remembered Nate driving, her first thought had been that he'd had a breakthrough. But maybe there was something she was missing here. Maybe being forced to confront his fear had pushed him backward, not forward.

Impossible to know without seeing him, and all this speculation was making her head ache. She closed her eyes and forced herself to think of something else, and after what felt like a long time she finally fell sleep.

The first thing she did when she woke the next morning was roll over and check the chair beside her bed. Again it was empty.

Disappointment descended on her, along with anxiety. She didn't understand what was going on. Then she pulled herself up in the bed and glanced toward the door and he was standing there.

"You're here," she said stupidly.

She waited for him to come to her side, to kiss her, but Nate didn't move.

"How's your arm?" he asked.

"It's fine. A little tender, but in the end I only needed a dozen or so stitches. Pretty amazing, huh?"

She smiled but he didn't smile back. All the doubts she'd

fought off in the small hours returned tenfold. She'd been telling herself there was an explanation, warning herself not to jump to conclusions, but now Nate was standing there looking cold and distant and she was afraid.

"Nate…? What's going on?"

Then her gaze moved beyond him and for the first time she saw her suitcase sitting just inside the door, her overnight bag set neatly beside it.

"I think I got everything. If there's anything else, I'll send it on," he said.

"I don't understand." Although she did. Of course she did.

"You should go home. Spend Christmas with your family."

"But…what about us?"

"You should go home," Nate repeated.

He was starting to really scare her. The flat, dead look in his eyes. The cool, resolved finality in his voice.

This was how he'd been with Jarvie. He'd cut Jarvie out of his life just as coldly. And now he was trying to do the same with her.

"What's going on, Nate? Talk to me. Whatever it is, we can work it out."

"There's nothing to work out. This should never have happened in the first place."

"Why not?"

"Because it was never going to work."

"That's not true, Nate—"

"I'm a mess. My life is screwed. I had no right dragging you into any of that."

"Your life is not a mess, Nate. You're recovering from major trauma, yes, but that doesn't mean your life is over. Every day you get better. The night sweats have stopped. And you drove,

Nate. You got in a car and drove. Doesn't that tell you that the way you're feeling has to shift?"

"Right. And then all the little bunny rabbits will skip down rainbow lane. It doesn't work like that, Elizabeth. Take it from someone who has lived with this shit for six months."

There was so much bitterness and anger in his voice. She set her jaw. He might not be able to see the light at the end of the tunnel, but she could. And she would continue to be the lamp holder for him on this if that was what it took to get him through.

"I know what you've gone through is hard. But you'll get there. I know you will. You'll get your old life back. I firmly believe it. We'll take it slowly, step by step. But it'll happen. We'll do it together. We'll do whatever it takes—"

"You don't know what you're talking about. You didn't hear her scream. You didn't watch them zip her into a body bag like a lump of meat. Nothing will ever be the same. *Nothing.*"

Elizabeth sat back against her pillows. She'd seen Nate's anxiety, his fear of driving, she'd seen him in the grip of night terrors. She'd watched him anesthetize himself with alcohol to take the edge off. She'd read about hypervigilance and depression and broken sleep. She'd seen the way he'd corralled himself into a corner, turning away from his old life and using his self-taught coping mechanisms to get through each day. She'd seen the pain and the shame and the fear.

But what she hadn't seen or understood until now was that underneath it all lay deep, soul-destroying guilt.

Nate blamed himself for his sister's death.

It was so simple, and yet she hadn't seen it until now.

He blamed himself. And he punished himself.

On some unconscious level, he welcomed the symptoms of his post-traumatic stress as due and just penance for his crime.

The anxiety, the inability to drive, the loss of his business—these were all fit punishments for a man who'd taken the life of the one person he loved above all others. The woman he'd raised almost as a daughter. The woman he'd strived so hard to provide for. The woman he would have died for.

Then Elizabeth had come along, and things had shifted, gotten better....

"You don't want to get better, do you?" she asked. "You think you deserve it. Don't you?"

"Spare me the pop psychology. What we had was a holiday fling. It's over. End of story. We both move on."

"No, Nate. What we *have* is a relationship, present tense, and I love you and you love me and the thought of having so much happiness within reach scares the hell out of you. The past few weeks, things have been changing for you, haven't they? You've been feeling better. Happier. More content. Which is why you sacrificed the business. God forbid you have Smartsell *and* me. One of those things had to go. And then you drove, breaking down another barrier and suddenly I'm on the chopping block, too.

"I thought you couldn't see the light at the end of the tunnel. But I was wrong, wasn't I? You *can* see it—you just don't think you deserve it. You won't let yourself have it. You want to keep paying penance for Olivia."

"This is bullshit. I'm selling the business because it's the right thing to do. And I'm ending things with you because there's no future in it."

"Answer me this, then, Nate. How did you get here today? Did you drive?"

It was a stab in the dark, but she knew Nate well enough to know that once he knew he could beat something, he wouldn't allow it to beat him. The expression on his face confirmed her guess and she smiled sadly.

"You're getting better. But it doesn't make you happy, does it?"

Nate's gaze fixed on a point over her shoulder. "I spoke to the travel agent on Main Street. There's a flight to London tomorrow night and there are plenty of seats."

"Were you speeding?"

He was taken off guard by her abrupt question and his gaze snapped back to her.

"What?"

"Were you speeding, the night of the accident?"

"No."

"Were you drunk? On drugs?"

He simply stared at her. She already knew the answer. Nate was too responsible to be so reckless.

"Did you try to steer out of the skid?"

Nate locked his jaw.

"Did you try to steer out of the skid?" she repeated.

"Yes."

"Tell me what else you could have done. Tell me what else you should have done to save her."

His jaw worked. There was so much guilt and anger in his eyes, so much grief....

"It was an accident, Nate. A horrible, pointless, unlucky accident. Not your fault. No one's fault. And I understand that that's maybe hard for you to deal with when you've lost someone you love so much, but you turning away from life is not going to bring Olivia back."

He dropped his head and lifted a hand to his face. For a moment she thought she'd finally gotten through to him, but when he lifted his head again the cool, distant expression was back in place.

"I hope your arm recovers quickly." He turned to leave.

"Nate. Don't you dare walk away from this."

He kept walking.

She threw off the covers and swung her legs over the edge of the bed. Her drip line got caught on the bed frame and she wasted precious seconds untangling it. When she was finally free to slide to her feet the abrupt movement sent a wave of dizziness washing over her.

She couldn't believe this was happening. By some miracle they'd found each other when, by rights, they should never have even crossed paths. She'd fallen in love with him, baggage and all. And now he was throwing their love away without even fighting for it.

Was he really so broken? And if so, what hope did she have of convincing him he deserved to be happy?

"Would Olivia want you to live like this, Nate? Would she?" she called after him.

She had no idea if he heard her. All she knew was that she felt as though she had just lost the most important battle of her life.

NATE TOLD HIMSELF HE'D done the right thing. All the way back to the island he told himself not to think about what Elizabeth had said. That she was upset and disappointed and that soon she'd forget about him and their time together.

He told himself that she didn't understand. That she had no idea. That things were better this way. Before she'd come along, he'd had it all worked out. And once she was gone, things would settle again. Go back to the way they were.

But she'd guessed he'd driven in to see her.

There was no way she could have known that he'd borrowed Trevor's car for a couple of hours yesterday and again this morning, forcing himself to work through his anxiety and the flashes of memory that washed over him. Forcing himself past the sweating and the shallow breathing until he was able to get in the car and put his hands on the steering wheel without hearing his sister pleading with him.

But Elizabeth had guessed. She'd known that once he'd proven to himself that he could drive if he had to, he wouldn't be able to let the fear beat him again.

He parked Trevor's car in the parking lot behind the pub and dropped off the keys at the bar. Then he walked down to the beach and headed home along the sand.

He'd become a master at blocking out things he didn't want to think about or feel over the past six months, but it was impossible to stop himself from mulling over what Elizabeth had said to him in her hospital room.

That he wanted to punish himself.

That he blamed himself for Olivia's death.

That he believed he didn't deserve to be happy.

He wanted to deny it all as a bunch of gobbledygook from the self-help section of the bookstore, but deep inside her words had struck a chord.

It *was* his fault that Olivia was dead, after all. He'd been driving. Her care—her life—had been in his hands. And he'd failed her.

Elizabeth could talk about luck and accidents and blame all she wanted, but the truth was immutable. It was his responsibility, all of it. Because of him, Olivia would never take the trip to Paris she'd always dreamed about. She'd never know if she could have made it into the School of Fashion and Textiles at the Royal Melbourne Institute of Technology. She'd never fall in love and marry and have a family of her own.

She was gone. His little sister.

And he was still here, not a scratch on him. Not even a freaking scar to show for the accident once the bruising had faded and the swelling gone down. He still had his wealth, his health, his life. Everything.

So, yeah. Maybe he did think there was a certain justice in

the night terrors and the flashbacks and the whole can't-get-behind-the-wheel-of-a-car thing. A life for a life. What could be more simple? More fitting?

The sun was hot as he walked from the beach into his street. There was beer in the fridge, he knew, and vodka in the freezer. He could numb himself with alcohol. Just to get through the next few days before Elizabeth was gone. And then it would be back to the usual. The days. The bar. The nights.

He entered the house through the back door. He'd cleaned the blood that first night—mopped it out of the kitchen and bathroom, soaked it out of the carpet in the hallway. It hadn't come out completely, of course. If he looked to his right, he'd see the dark stain where Elizabeth had collapsed in the hall.

He didn't look. He went to the fridge and grabbed a beer. Then he sat at the kitchen table and drank it down, staring at the wall and willing himself not to think.

Would Olivia want you to live like this, Nate?

He should never have hooked up with Elizabeth. He should never have let himself get involved with her or her quest to find her father. He should never have sought comfort and solace in her arms.

Would Olivia want you to live like this?

He slammed the bottle down onto the table and beer frothed over the top. He swore, then stood and went to the fridge. Clearly, reinforcements were called for. Beer wasn't going to cut it today.

He opened the freezer and found himself staring at ice cream and frozen vegetables and meat. Only then did he remember that Lizzy had relegated his vodka bottle to the cupboard. She'd claimed it was because they needed the freezer space, but he'd known it was part of her quietly determined effort to encourage him to drink less.

He crossed the kitchen and pulled open the cabinet over the counter. He could see the vodka bottle, lying on its side along the back, but his gaze was drawn to the pink-and-white plastic bag of marshmallows sitting at the front of the shelf. A sticky note was attached to the bag, Lizzy's old-school cursive script curling across the small square of paper: *Don't even think about finishing these without me!!!*

Like a physical blow, clarity tensed his gut and made him take a step backward.

He would never see Elizabeth again. He'd ensured that with his words and actions today. There would be no more of her laughter and dry looks and calm certainty. He would never touch the silk of her skin or taste her kisses or see the warm, clear light in her eyes. He would never walk into a room and smell her perfume and know she was nearby. As far as he was concerned, it would be as though she had died that night in his bloodstained hallway. She would become nothing but a memory.

But she wouldn't really be dead. She would be in London, living her life. He imagined how it might be—Lizzy at school teaching her kids, finding her way again on the other side of the world. Her tan fading, along with her memories of him. And then, eventually, she would meet someone else and fall in love. She'd get married and have children. And some other lucky bastard would get to sleep with her each night and grow old with her and comfort her when she needed it and make her laugh when she was sad and infuriate and challenge and adore her.

He sucked in a ragged breath.

Jesus, he wanted to be that lucky bastard. He wanted the peace of waking in her arms. He wanted the joy of being inside her, her body warm against his. He wanted to watch her bloom as she discovered all the things about herself she'd been too scared and dutiful to acknowledge. He wanted the happiness she offered so easily, so openly.

He wanted a future full of hope and possibility, not this quarter-life of regret and fear and loneliness.

The moment he acknowledged his own desire, the old guilt rose inside him. How could he open himself to so much happiness when Olivia was gone? How could he allow himself to live fully without her? If he picked up the threads of his life, if he kept growing Smartsell and he allowed himself to have Elizabeth, if he could truly *live* again, it would be as though he was denying Olivia ever existed. As though her death meant nothing to him.

You turning away from life is not going to bring Olivia back.

Nate closed his eyes. He knew Lizzy was right. Olivia was dead. He missed her like crazy, would probably continue to miss her like crazy every day for the rest of his life, but all the guilt and pain and self-flagellating in the world was not going to bring her back.

The bottom line was that she was gone. And he was not.

And he didn't want to keep living like this. He didn't want to be a victim of his own memories. He didn't want to let fear control his world.

But most of all he didn't want to let Lizzy go. In a few short weeks she had turned his life upside down. He needed her. He wanted her. He loved her. And maybe it made him a bad brother and a weak, selfish bastard, but so be it.

He chose life. He chose Lizzy.

If she'd still have him.

He was on his feet in a split second, out the door a heartbeat after that. He broke into a run. He'd go back to the pub, ask Trevor for his car again. Lizzy would still be at the hospital. And if she wasn't, he'd track her down. Wherever she'd gone.

His step faltered as he registered the beaten-up four-wheel drive parked out the front of his house. A woman was sliding carefully out of the passenger seat, a man on crutches hovering protectively at her side.

"Lizzy," he said, stopping in his tracks.

Her head came up and the look she gave him was pure defiant challenge.

"Don't bother telling me to go away, Nathan, because I'm not going anywhere. It's taken me half my life to work out what I want and no way am I walking away from it now. So I don't care what you say, I'm staying, and I'm going to keep loving you, and there's nothing you can do about it."

He closed the distance between them in three strides. Then he pulled her into his arms, resting his cheek against the crown of her head, breathing in the smell of her.

Elizabeth was very still in his arms. He pressed a kiss to the top of her head. Slowly her body relaxed and she wrapped her good arm around him.

"This had better mean what I think it does," she said, her voice muffled by the front of his shirt.

He smiled slightly.

"That was your cue to say something reassuring. In case you missed it," she said.

He loosened his arms enough to look into her face. "I love you."

She bit her lip. He cupped her face and brushed his thumb along her cheekbone.

"Did I mess up my line?" he asked.

"No. It was perfect. I just thought I was going to have to wrestle you to the ground before I got you to admit it."

"I want this, Lizzy. I want you. I want to make it work. I know it's been tough. It's probably going to be tough again. I'll go back to my therapist, talk to my doctor about medication. I'll do what I can. But—"

She pressed her fingers to his lips. "My love doesn't come with *buts*. It just is. Whatever happens, we'll deal with it."

She looked into his eyes, her own very steady and certain.

"Lizzy," he said, but the rest of the things he wanted to say got caught in his throat.

She smiled and stood on her toes to press a kiss to his lips.

"I know."

Epilogue

Six months later

ELIZABETH CHECKED HER watch and stood on her toes again, trying to see around the people standing in front of them at the international arrivals gate.

Nate put his arm around her shoulders. "Relax, Lizzy. They'll walk through the doors, we'll see them. It's a pretty simple process."

This was their second trip to the airport for the week. Her grandparents had arrived on Monday, flying in easy stages from London for her grandmother's benefit. No one had been more surprised than Elizabeth when they announced they were coming to visit. She and Nate had already planned to fly to London for their wedding, but her grandparents' announcement had led to a hurried reorganizing of events, the upshot of which was that two weeks from now, she and Nate would walk down the aisle at a beautiful Gothic revival church in Albert Park with both her grandparents and her father in attendance.

She'd be lying if she said she wasn't worried about how her grandparents and Sam would cope with coming face-to-face after so many years and so many mistakes on both sides.

But Sam was a part of her life now whether her grandparents liked it or not so they were going to have to work things out between them.

"Remind me again how long we're going to have all these houseguests?" Nate said.

"Grandmama and Grandpa for three weeks. Violet for four."

He pulled a face. "That seems like a pretty long time."

She knew what he was thinking about—having her grandparents in residence definitely put a damper on their sex life.

"We could always sneak away for a weekend. Go down to the island."

His eyes lit up. "Keep talking."

"We could hole up in the studio and not come out all weekend," she said.

Nate lowered his head to whisper in her ear. "And then?"

She lowered her own voice and turned to face him, looping her arms loosely around his neck. "Then you could help me grade all the papers for Year Nine English."

"Hmm. Not quite what I had in mind."

He was smiling and she reached up to smooth his hair.

"Let me think about it. See if I can come up with a little something else," she said.

"You do that."

His phone rang and she let her arms drop so he could move away to take it. She could tell by the way his gaze grew distant that it was a business call. He'd started back at Smartsell four months ago, working part-time at first and gradually increasing his hours until he was fully back into the swing of things. To say that Jarvie was happy was an understatement. He was like an overly affectionate dog when he was around Nate, hugely grateful to have his old friend back on deck.

It hadn't all been smooth sailing. Nate had had trouble

sleeping again when he returned to his therapist, the therapy stirring up difficult memories. There had been bouts of withdrawal and bad temper, too, in the early days. He'd become so used to being on his own, to keeping his own counsel. But they had both persevered, and things had slowly shifted. He was still uncomfortable with night driving—he made himself do it, but she was always aware that it was an effort, a sort of trial-by-endurance that he made himself face. She knew he was still prone to the occasional anxiety attack, but they were getting better, too.

And last month, they'd cleaned out Olivia's room. It had been heartbreaking, packing away the remnants of a life that had barely started. It had been Nate's decision, reached in his own time. Elizabeth had kept aside a few things— some soft toys, some cushions Olivia had sewn, a handful of well-thumbed children's books. One day, when she and Nate had children, she wanted them to have a connection to their aunt.

"Lizzy."

Elizabeth started out of her introspection to glance at Nate.

"Is it just me, or is that what's-his-name?" he asked as he pocketed his phone.

She followed his sight line and blinked.

What on earth was Martin doing here? Then a familiar redhead appeared over his shoulder. Martin and Violet. *Together?*

It was such an absurd idea she laughed. It must be a coincidence.

Then Violet looked up and caught Elizabeth's eye, and the guilt and defiance and hope in her friend's face made Elizabeth press her fingers to her lips with shock.

"Let me guess—that's Violet?" Nate said close to her ear.

"Yes. But they hate each other, Nate. They used to fight

like cat and dog. She used to call him Droopy Drawers and he could barely say her name without sneering."

Nate shrugged. "Stranger things have happened, Lizzy."

She met his eyes. There was so much love and understanding there that she couldn't help but smile.

"Yes, they have, haven't they?" Their hands found each other, fingers weaving together.

Thank God he'd forgiven himself. Thank God he'd given them a chance.

"Come on," he said. "Let's go hear their story."

* * * * *

COMING NEXT MONTH

Available September 28, 2010

REQUEST YOUR FREE BOOKS!

2 FREE NOVELS
PLUS 2
FREE GIFTS!

HARLEQUIN®

Blaze™

Red-hot reads!

HARLEQUIN®

A Romance

FOR EVERY MOOD™

Spotlight on

Inspirational

Wholesome romances
that touch the heart and soul.

See the next page
to enjoy a sneak peek from
the Love Inspired® inspirational series.

*See below for a sneak peek at
our inspirational line, Love Inspired®.
Introducing HIS HOLIDAY BRIDE
by bestselling author Jillian Hart*

Autumn Granger gave her horse rein to slide toward the town's new sheriff.

"Hey, there." The man in a brand-new Stetson, black T-shirt, jeans and riding boots held up a hand in greeting. He stepped away from his four-wheel drive with "Sheriff" in black on the doors and waded through the grasses. "I'm new around here."

"I'm Autumn Granger."

"Nice to meet you, Miss Granger. I'm Ford Sherman, from Chicago." He knuckled back his hat, revealing the most handsome face she'd ever seen. Big blue eyes contrasted with his sun-tanned complexion.

"I'm guessing you haven't seen much open land. Out here, you've got to keep an eye on cows or they're going to tear your vehicle apart."

"What?" He whipped around. Sure enough, mammoth black-and-white creatures had started to gnaw on his four-wheel drive. They clustered like a mob, mouths and tongues and teeth bent on destruction. One cow tried to pry the wiper off the windshield, another chewed on the side mirror. Several leaned through the open window, licking the seats.

"Move along, little dogie." He didn't know the first thing about cattle.

The entire herd swiveled their heads to study him curiously. Not a single hoof shifted. The animals soon returned to chewing, licking, digging through his possessions.

Autumn laughed, a warm and wonderful sound. "Thanks,

I needed that." She then pulled a bag from behind her saddle and waved it at the cows. "Look what I have, guys. Cookies."

Cows swung in her direction, and dozens of liquid brown eyes brightened with cookie hopes. As she circled the car, the cattle bounded after her. The earth shook with the force of their powerful hooves.

"Next time, you're on your own, city boy." She tipped her hat. The cowgirl stayed on his mind, the sweetest thing he had ever seen.

*Will Ford be able to stick it out in the country
to find out more about Autumn?
Find out in HIS HOLIDAY BRIDE
by bestselling author Jillian Hart,
available in October 2010
only from Love Inspired®.*